Uncle Fred Wilson is a retired microbiologist

that lives in Little Rock, Arkansas.

He has also written:

SLOW MOTION EMERGENCY
&
ALIZARIN ANGEL

The Man Who Dropped In

Chapter 1

It was taking Kenny nearly forever to get started. It was late summer and there would be plenty of ripe persimmons down along the creek, and plenty of unripe ones which would ripen up later. He had filled his water bottle and sprayed himself down with insect repellant. He was just waiting for Jimbo to get back from baseball practice. He had told his mother that Jimbo knew where to go and could catch up with him later, but she insisted that he wait. She had always impressed upon them to be on the safe side if you were going out in the deep woods. Kenny had a short ladder for getting higher in the tree, but he would need Jimbo to hold the ladder if he was going to climb it. Kenny was almost 15, and too old for the little league Jimbo played in. Jimbo was 13 and it was the last year he could play. Their mother, Irene, was widowed and supported them by managing the Pine Valley Store. It had been a café at one time, but the business had dwindled down to where she only served coffee, iced tea and sweet rolls. She was hoping that the boys would bring back enough persimmons to bake a few pies, which she could serve to her morning customers. They would welcome the change from sweet rolls while the persimmons held out. Kenny had filled two pint bottles with water and brought four granola bars; two apiece for himself and Jimbo to snack on. Kenny had blue eyes, sandy hair and wore glasses for his moderate myopia. He was five feet eight and still growing. He wore a Dallas Cowboys t-shirt, jeans and sneakers for venturing into the creek bottom.

"What's up Big Bro," Jimbo called out as he entered the store.

"Just waiting for you, man." Kenny replied. "I've got some zip-lock bags, and snacks and water. If you don't need to change I'm ready when you are."

"All right, let's head out," Jimbo shot back. He looked a lot like

Kenny but was six inches shorter. He was wearing jeans and sneakers with a red Coca-Cola t-shirt. They walked straight out the front door and crossed the road, going almost due west into the mixed hardwood and pine forest. There was a trail worn into the woods from many feet that led to the blackberry bushes and persimmon trees in the bottoms. Jimbo had been four years old when their father, Patrick Webb, had been killed in a car accident, and he didn't remember his dad very well. Kenny remembered him better, but they rarely talked about him. There had just been Irene and the boys for most of their lives. The cooing of doves was the only sound they heard as they made their way.

It took about twenty minutes to reach the pair of persimmon trees, deep in the creek bottom. As they got closer they suddenly saw a large bird flap its wings and fly a short distance before perching in a pine tree.

"Buzzard," Kenny said.

"Must be a dead animal around. You smell anything?" Jimbo replied.

"Nope, just the mosquito repellant. Wait, what's that over there? Looks like a rag or something." Jimbo walked towards where Kenny was pointing.

"There's somebody's foot." Jimbo whispered. "Let's look closer."

"You look closer, I'm staying right here," Kenny insisted. There was a man lying in the brush. Jimbo inched closer and closer to the man. His right pants leg had a large bloodstain. Jimbo looked closely at his head. One side of his face was bruised and had several cuts. Jimbo noticed that he was breathing. "He's breathing," he said to Kenny. Kenny moved closer until he was right behind Jimbo.

It appeared that the man had laid some pine boughs on the ground where he was lying. He wore one sock- on his right foot, and his shirt was torn in several places. Kenny leaned in and

2

spoke, "Are you hurt bad?"

For several seconds the man panted, then rasped, "I'm not sure." The boys helped him sit up, then Kenny handed him a water bottle. He drank most of it, then he said, "Thanks, I'm so glad to see somebody."

Kenny handed him a granola bar, and he bit off a piece and chewed for a minute or two. "Where did you come from?" Kenny inquired.

"I'm not sure of that either, and I'm not sure what my name is." he managed to rasp, "Can you help me?"

"Sure," Kenny replied, "We'll get you some help."

The man looked up and studied their faces. "Reach in my hip pocket and get my billfold," he requested. Jimbo pulled out the billfold. "Is my driver's license in there?"

Jimbo said, "No, there's nothing in here but a twenty-dollar bill."

"Huh, guess they didn't want me to be broke if I didn't die."

"Can you walk?" asked Kenny.

The man sighed, "Just barely, that ankle hurts pretty bad- can't put my weight on it." They noticed that under the sock, the ankle was badly swollen.

Kenny asked, "Could you ride a horse if we borrowed one?"

"Yeah, I guess- can you tell me what year this is?" he replied.

"Nineteen ninety-four, July the fourteenth." said Kenny. "Jimbo, why don't you stay here with him and I'll go borrow a horse from Perry."

"Bring back some more granola bars- chocolate if she's got any," Jimbo replied. Kenny trotted off up the trail.

When Irene saw Kenny emerge from the woods she noticed he was heading in the direction of Perry's place and she wanted to know what was going on. As she left the store she told her associate, Dotty, to keep an eye on things until she returned. She wasn't in the best shape at thirty-seven, but she arrived at Perry's

3

in time to hear her son asking to borrow a horse.

"What's going on, Kenny, where's your brother?"

"He's OK, Mom, he's down in the woods. We found a feller down there and he's hurt. I'm borrowing Gordy so he can ride back, he can't walk."

"All right, I'm coming with you." She followed Kenny out the back door and down to the corral. Perry was close behind.

Perry said, "Let's put a saddle on ol' Gordy, it'll be his good deed for the month."

"Mom, could you get a couple granola bars so we can reward Gordy and give one to the feller, he hasn't eaten in a while." Kenny requested.

Irene said, "Oh lord…don't leave without me." When she arrived back at the store she put the granola bars in the left pocket of her jeans and her twenty-two derringer in the right, just to be on the safe side. Perry, Kenny and she, along with Gordy, headed down the trail. "How tall is this person, Kenny? There's low hanging branches down here."

"Oh, he's just under six foot, but he'll have to lean over in a couple places. We need to get hold of Doc Barnes. I hope he's home. The man's got a lot of cuts and bruises and his ankle's all swole up. Doc'll know what he needs." Kenny explained.

"How did he get here?" Perry asked.

"He doesn't know," Kenny answered, "He's probably had a concussion- his head's all bruised up."

Irene was somewhat shaken when she saw the man who was sitting next to Jimbo. She tried not to let her imagination run wild but she couldn't help wondering at the whole scenario. She put one knee to the ground and spoke softly to the man, "I'm Irene Webb, and we're going to get you some help."

He replied, "Thanks, ma'am, I appreciate it. I'll pay you back, I really will."

4

"Don't worry about that now, it's OK. What can we call you?" she asked.

He thought for a moment, "Just call me Bud. That is, if you don't already have a Bud."

"No, that will be fine." She said. "Can you stand up?"

"Yeah, can you guys help me up?" Kenny and Jimbo held his shoulders so he could stand.

Perry led the horse closer. He said, "This is Gordy, he's real gentle, we'll just take it nice and slow." Bud reached up and held onto the horn. He lifted his left foot into the stirrup and Perry and the boys helped him swing his injured right leg over the saddle. "You'll need to support that foot or all the blood will drain into it." Perry advised. They helped him get his toes into the stirrup. He bit into the granola bar and chewed. It seemed like the best thing he's ever tasted.

Four local people, one horse, one injured man- Irene was thinking about how life is full of the unexpected. She unwrapped a granola bar and held it out for Gordy. He eagerly accepted it and chewed it with obvious pleasure. As expected, Bud had to lower his head to the horse's neck several times as they made their way back to Pine Valley. They stopped so everyone could catch their breath. "Wait," Irene said, "Where's Kenny."

Jimbo said, "Well, we came down here to pick persimmons, so he's picking some."

"Oh, yeah, I almost forgot. When he gets back, tell him to put them in the fridge."

When they came into the clearing at the end of the trail, Dr. Barnes was sitting on one of the lawn chairs in front of the store. Perry's wife, Loretta had called him to report the news. Perry helped the man down from the saddle. Dr. Barnes said, "I'm a doctor, sit down in that chair and let me have a look at you." He looked closely at the man's head, then leaned over and looked at

his swollen ankle. When he raised up he said, "I can't do anything for you here, I'll have to take you to the clinic in Dequeen.
Can I borrow your boy Mrs. Webb? We'll get him in my car and run him down there. We'll take care of you. What's your name?"

"I'm really not sure. You can call me Bud for the time being."

"OK, Bud, let me pull my car over here and we'll get going." Jimbo opened the door of Doc's Oldsmobile and the man called Bud sat back into the passenger seat. Jimbo helped him lift his right foot onto the floor board and shut the door, then he got in the back seat, and Doc headed east.

When they had gone, Irene was asking herself if this was real or just a strange dream. Kenny soon returned with a one-gallon bag full of ripe persimmons and the other bag nearly full of green ones- they would ripen up in a day or two. She filled Kenny in on what his brother, Doc, and Bud were doing. "I wonder what kind of medical care he can get having amnesia and nobody knows whether he's got any medical insurance or knows anything else about him? He had a billfold in the pocket of his pants- all it had in it was a twenty dollar bill. Whoever left him there took every kind of ID that he had, but left him with twenty bucks. Isn't that kind of strange?" Kenny asked.

"I agree" his mom replied, "Why don't you help me take the seeds out of these persimmons while I make some pie crusts. I've got to do something to get my mind off this situation."

"You're not mad about us bringing that feller up here, are you?" Kenny asked.

"No, as a matter of fact, Jesus made it perfectly clear what to do in a case like this. You did exactly what you should have done. I'm proud of you boys." Irene replied.

"It's funny," Kenny mused, "It seems like what happened to him was just what happened to the feller on the road to Jericho, except he got left with twenty bucks."

"Well, I just hope it turns out that he's somebody we can trust-not a mean person like so many these days." Irene sighed.

Kenny said, "I don't know, I just have this feeling that he's just a regular feller with a job and a family and he just had bad luck and ran into some real bad people."

"I hope you're right," Irene replied.

On the way to Dequeen Bud was the first to speak. "I'll pay you guys back someday."

"Don't worry about that," Dr. Barnes said, "We've got to get you healthy before anything else. How long ago did you regain consciousness?"

"Oh, I don't know, maybe several hours. When I woke up I was just lying on the damp ground. I just laid there for a while because I was so tired. My head hurt, and when I tried to stand up I could barely walk because my ankle was either broke or sprained. I was so glad to see those boys."

"So you were walking before you laid down?"

"I guess I was walking."

"Were you walking upstream or downstream?"

"Upstream, I think."

"You'd usually go downstream if you were lost."

"The vegetation was heavier downstream."

"That would make sense," Doc replied.

Jimbo asked, "Could he have been walking for several hours and not remember? I mean, wouldn't you have to be conscious to be walking?"

Doc replied, "Well yes and no. There's such a thing as semiconscious. Like when you're sleepwalking. That could very well have been what happened. Bud, do you know what you did for a living?"

"Hmm, I seem to be farther back. I mean, before I did anything for a living," he answered.

7

"Ah, all right," said Doc, "You've got more early memory than you do recent memory. Well, we won't worry about that for now. We'll take some time and let your brain cells heal, then we can talk some more later. Right now we'll work on your injuries."

It was quarter to six when they got to the clinic. Irene had called ahead to let them know they were on their way. A young male resident was waiting by the front desk when they came. He showed them into an examining room right away. "I'm Dr. Ahmed Solomon," he said.

"I'm Dr. Herschel Barnes, I don't practice anymore, but I'm seeing to this man's care. He's a 'John Doe' patient, we're calling him 'Bud' for now. And this young man is Jimbo Webb. Along with his brother, they rescued this man from the creek bottom about ten miles from here."

Dr. Solomon had him remove his clothes and then checked his eyes and ears. He asked Dr. Barnes to check for ticks. "We'll suture those lacerations, but I want to take some x-rays, and we can't do that 'til tomorrow. Can he spend the night here?"

"We'll take him back with us and bring him back in the morning," said Dr. Barnes, "Go ahead and get all his vital signs, Pine Valley is a real tight little community. I guess if you were going to get abandoned somewhere, it's a good place to be."

Dr. Solomon laughed, "I know what you mean. I think I might like to be the doctor in a place like this."

A half dozen people were sitting around at the store in Pine Valley discussing the stranger who had come to town. There were a few used pieces of clothing that people had donated sitting on the counter. They were discussing how much money it would take to supply Bud with some socks and underwear. A man named Jim said, "Kenny said he's about my size which would be size thirty-four underwear. Let's get him two pairs of underwear and two pairs of socks. Irene have you got any?"

8

"I believe I do," she replied, "Six bucks will cover it." Jim handed her a five and Perry handed her a dollar.

When Doc and Jimbo returned with the injured man Irene said, "He can sleep on the couch in the pool room tonight if that's ok, Doc."

"That will be fine," Dr. Barnes replied, "Have you got a quilt and a pillow handy?"

Loretta said, "I've got a quilt and a pillow he can use."

Bud had bandages on his head and both arms. His right ankle was heavily wrapped. Doc and Jim helped him through the door into the pool room and over to the couch where he sat down and leaned back.

"I don't know how to thank you folks," He said.

"That's ok," Irene assured him, I'm getting some supper together for the boys and us. You just take it easy 'til it's ready."

Doc said, "You folks come out here in the store for a minute. I need to tell you something." When they were all in the front of the store, he began, "I think it would be a good idea if we all didn't talk about this for the time being. This man is lost and he has amnesia. I'm going to ask Judge James to help us. He can deal with the man's legal status and I'll deal with his medical care. We're both retired so we've got the time to work with him. I know it's exciting, I know it's interesting, but it wouldn't be in his best interest to be telling all of our neighbors about this. Someone may have tried to kill him and we don't know why. I know we all want to help and we will. But just help me keep a lid on things until we get this all sorted out so we can get him back where he belongs. Are you all with me on this?" They murmured their agreement. "All right then, I'll be back in the morning to carry him down to the clinic and take some x-rays. You all have a nice evening, and thanks for your understanding."

9

Chapter 2

Irene was up early the next morning baking persimmon pies. When she came in the store, the man was sitting watching TV. "I hope you got some sleep last night," she asked him.

"Yes, thanks, I was pretty tired. Lots better than sleeping on the bare ground," he replied, "When your boys found me yesterday, I was never so glad to see humans in all my life."

"I'll bet," said Irene, "I'll put some coffee on and you can have a piece of pie if you want. Folks will be coming in pretty soon."

Bud was chatting with Jim and Lisa Tanner when Doc arrived. Jim had just asked Bud if there was anything they could get for him. The only thing he could think of was licorice. Doc said, "Hey, that's a little bit of your memory coming back. That was the only thing you could think of at the moment, but in time you'll think of other things. Well, let's go on back to the clinic and get you x-rayed."

Jim said, "I'll find you some licorice, I'm sure they've got it either in Dequeen or Broken Bow."

On the way to Dequeen Doc asked Bud how he felt. "Well, I feel a whole lot better now than I did yesterday." Bud shook his head, "These folks are just so nice. It gives me the feeling that everything's going to come out all right."

"Sure it will," Doc replied, "Small town people really know how to cooperate. Because they all know each other they're not afraid to help each other out. Have you had any thoughts about what kind of work you might have done?"

Bud said, "I don't know, but I had this feeling when Irene was in the kitchen, baking…that I might have done something like that. Maybe not for pay, but just to, you know, just help out."

"That's good, it'll come back to you little by little. Have you been having any pain?"

"My ankle was hurting but it seems to have gone down. My head aches off and on."

"You aren't allergic to any pain killers, are you? Oh hell, I'm sorry, you wouldn't know."

Bud laughed, "No, I have no idea. Well, if it doesn't get any worse, maybe I won't need to take anything."

"Let's hope so," said Dr. Barnes. "I took the liberty of contacting Judge James. He retired from the bench after twenty years and practiced law before that."

"Sounds fine with me," Bud replied.

"He would do a lot better than I could about searching out your background. Of course he would be very discreet to avoid having the wrong kind of people find out about you."

"Who would they be? If you don't mind my asking."

"Well, it's very likely that they were on the wrong side of the law. If you had been on the wrong side, there would have been bulletins out with your description. Plus you wouldn't have been hiding in a creek bottom is southeast Oklahoma."

"I thought this was Arkansas."

"Just barely, Pine Valley is just a stone's throw from the border. There wouldn't be a sign except on a paved road. Anyway, it seems as though somebody tried to, at least, do you harm, and we need to find out why. Albert James is somebody you can trust to help you without letting on to where you are and what you're doing."

Along the road to Dequeen there were five houses, a cemetery, and three small businesses.

Mack Howser and his wife Hazel had a place called Trailers and Alterations. Mack made and traded general purpose flat-bed trailers and Hazel was a seamstress. She could make garments out of nearly any material available. Deer hunters would bring her tanned deerskins that she would make into beautiful vests and jackets. They would bring along an old garment that fit well on the person and she did the rest. Mack also did general welding, both arc and acetylene.

Chester's Wood Shop was a little ways past the Howsers. Chester was a retired deputy sheriff. He made bird houses, bat houses, clocks, shoe racks, hat racks, and small carvings of cowboys, horses, and Christmas nativity sets.

The other business on the highway was Bill's Used Tires. Bill had a large metal building filled with hundreds of tires. He bought most of them from salvage yards and many of them were nearly new. If you needed a tire of any size, Bill would usually have it. And he could mount and balance them too.

"You know, I've never heard of persimmons, before," Bud offered, "But that pie was really good. Isn't that the clinic right ahead?"

"Yep, you're doing better already. You must have come from somewhere that they don't have persimmons," Doc commented.

Dr. Barnes and Dr. Solomon looked closely at the x-rays. The skull wasn't fractured, but the brain had been severely injured. Concussions take a lot of time to heal and some people never recover from a brain injury. The ankle had some hair-line fractures and soft tissue damage. Bud was fitted with a walking cast. The consensus was to keep his weight off of it until it had a chance to heal. They loaned him a pair of crutches to use until his ankle healed up.

"What do I owe you for all this?" Bud asked.

Doc Barnes said, "Well, look at it this way, you're in no condition to be paying anybody for the time being. Once you're back on your feet we won't hesitate to ask for your help with things a young, strong man can do that older ones can't. How does that sound?"

12

Bud stuck out his right hand, "It's a deal, Doc." He also shook Dr. Solomon's hand.

On the way back to Pine Valley Doc asked, "Feel like meeting Judge James?"

"Sure, although I'm not sure if there is anything I can remember now that I couldn't yesterday," Bud replied.

"That's okay, we'll just talk things over; I'm sure there are some avenues the judge can explore due to his expertise with the law," Doc said.

"I'm just wondering," Bud began, "How did this town get the name, 'Dequeen?'"

"Well, it happened like this, a business from the Netherlands bought a big tract of land they could get timber from. The head of the company spelled his name, 'D-E-G-O-E-I-J-E-N' The local people couldn't pronounce that so they anglicized it to De Queen and then to Dequeen."

Judge James lived just outside of Foreman. Doc pulled into the yard and helped Bud onto his crutches. Lindy, the judge's wife, met them at the door. "Oh hello, Doc, come on in," she said, "Albert is in the living room."

"This is Bud, Lindy, our lost traveler," said Dr. Barnes.

"C'mon in and sit down, folks," said the judge.

"I'll get you some coffee," said Mrs. James.

The Judge started, "Well, you were just west of Pine Valley and you were injured- no shoes and no ID.?"

Dr. Barnes said, "He had a billfold with a twenty dollar bill- nothing else. Bud, do any names come to mind?"

"You know, it's kind of funny, I think I've got more than one name, if that makes any sense," Bud replied.

Doc said, "You mean like a two-part first name, or known by more than one name? Like an alias."

"Yeah, like my name got changed," Bud replied.

"I see," said the judge, "that might very well be a clue. About how many people might know you by your name after it changed?"

"Not very many, I don't think. Maybe a dozen or so," said Bud, "When those boys found me I was laying on some pine boughs, but I remember laying on the cold damp ground for the just the longest time. It was like all I knew was that I was alive, and I was just glad I was in some woods and not in a desert."

Judge James said, "Ah yes, it doesn't seem like a lot but it was something to be thankful for. I've noticed from your accent and the kind of phrases you use that you must have lived in the North. Do you remember harsh winters as opposed to mild ones?"

"I can't really remember," Bud replied, "but I have more of a fear of being cold than being hot."

"That may be helpful," the judge said. "I'll tell you what we'll do. We'll take your fingerprints. I'll get in touch with the state Attorney General. He'll try to find out if the Justice Department has any record of you in its files."

Bud said, "You know, I used to think the FBI could find out who you were just from your fingerprints."

"Oh, yes," the judge replied, "they had us all believing that for years. It turns out that all they can really do is just compare one set of prints with another and tell if they're the same. It's a wonderful tool, but you can't exactly put them in alphabetical or numerical order. But if there is somebody missing in one of their witness protection programs, it might narrow it down to where they have a finite number to look at."

"I think I see what you're driving at," said Bud, "Say, could I play your piano?"

"Actually it's an organ," said Judge James, "But sure, feel free."

14

As Bud made his way to the organ, Mrs. James entered the room with a tray. She set it down on the small coffee table. Her curiosity was piqued to see Bud sitting down at the organ.

Doc called out, "Hey, I'll bet twenty dollars you can't play that thing."

"You're on," Bud replied. He proceeded to play a scale and a few chords, then he played Red River Valley with a rock beat to it. Then he said, "Aw, come on Doc, you knew I had twenty dollars."

Doc laughed, "Well now you have forty dollars."

Bud returned to the sofa and Mrs. James handed him a cup of coffee. "Cream and sugar?" she asked.

"Just cream," he uttered, then his eyebrows raised.

"Yeah," said Doc, "Your memory's coming back in small pieces. OK, here's a question, what did you call your mom?"

Bud took a sip of coffee. "I think I just called her Mom. But my grandmother, was Big Mama."

"Now we're getting somewhere," Doc said, "Did you spend a lot of time with your grandmother?"

"I might have," Bud replied, "I don't know for sure."

"Like maybe your mom worked," said the judge, "and your grandmother helped out."

"I feel like there's some possibilities but nothing definite," said Bud with a sigh.

"Well," said Albert James, "let's just let it go until I find out what I can from the federal boys. I'm friends with the AG in Little Rock and he'll help us if he can."

Dr. Barnes said, "We know you came from up north, originally. You like licorice, and you take cream in your coffee."

Lindy said, "And you can play keyboards. Now where can we get the fingerprints done? The courthouse in Dequeen?"

"That's the closest," said the judge.

15

When they arrived back in Pine Valley, Doc left Bud off at the store. Irene greeted him when he came in. "Are you ready for some lunch?" she asked.

"Ready as I'll ever be, thanks. You know, if you've got the stuff to make pizza, I can make it for you sometime," he said.

"I might take you up on that," Irene replied, "as soon as the boys get here we'll eat. By the way, Jim Tanner found some Twizzlers at the Walmart in Dequeen, so I got a five pound box."

"Oh, yay," Bud enthused, "I think that's the kind I usually get."

There was a long Formica topped table in the store that served as a dinner table. Folding chairs were there for seating purposes. Irene carried in four plates of black-eyed peas, pork chops and corn bread. Kenny and Jimbo soon arrived. Nobody spoke for several minutes as they ate.

Bud said, "The kind of corn bread I ate when I was a kid was sort of sweet, but what I've had as a grownup isn't sweet."

"That's because," Irene mused, "Black people and northern white people put sugar in the batter. So that suggests that you came from up north, but you've lived down south since then." There was a long pause, then Irene said, "Now tell me about this pizza."

Bud put his fork down. "Well first you have to have bread dough. You can either make it yourself with flour, warm water and yeast, or you can get frozen bread dough and thaw out one loaf- which is the size for a large pizza."

"We could make the dough easy enough," Irene commented. "What else do you need?"

Bud continued, "Tomato paste, can of olives, can of mushrooms, an onion, mozzarella cheese, pepperoni or sausage. That's about it."

"You can do this?" Kenny inquired.

"Anybody could do it," said Bud

16

Irene said, "Tell you what, if I get you the stuff, you can make us a pizza."

"You're on," Bud replied, "but where can you get that stuff?"

"Same place we got the licorice," said Irene. She rose and went to the cash register, then returned. She placed a package of Twizzlers on the table. "There's dessert."

"Oh man," Bud exclaimed, "I'm ready for that as soon as I finish this pork chop."

When they had finished eating Bud opened the pack of Twizzlers and offered everybody a stick of licorice. Bud closed his eyes as he bit into the licorice. He sighed as he chewed. Irene wasn't interested. Kenny tried a bite and decided he didn't like it. Jimbo liked it and Kenny said, "Here, you can have the rest of mine."

Irene said, "That's how it is with licorice, some people don't like it, but the ones that do, really like it."

Kenny said, "How did things go with Judge James?"

"Well, just a few things. He took my fingerprints and he's going to talk to the state attorney general. I always thought you could find somebody's identity from their fingerprints, but it's not true. Fingerprints just prove whether or not a certain person touched something. But if they come up with a list of people that I might be, then my prints could match up. But, on another note, the judge had a Thomas Organ and I played it."

"Oh, cool," Jimbo exclaimed, "you're a musician!"

"Well, maybe not a musician," Bud answered, "but I can play."

"Let me think," Irene mused, "Don't you boys know somebody who's got a keyboard?"

"Yeah, Loretta's brother has a synthesizer," Kenny said, "He probably wouldn't mind Bud playing it."

"I have an idea," Irene said, "Jim and Scotty, and them, have a jam on Saturday afternoon. If Fred would let us borrow the keyboard, we could have the jam here in the store."

Kenny laughed, "Yeah, and of course they'll want cold drinks and coffee while they're here."

"Well, so what," Irene responded, "We could set out some free snacks, and everybody would be happy."

"Oh, don't get me wrong," Kenny replied, "I think it's a great idea."

They sat and talked for about an hour, then Bud said, "If you guys don't mind, I'd kinda like to lie down for a while, I'm pretty tired."

"Oh, no problem," Irene replied, "you need to rest up and get your strength and health back." She went to get him a pillow and a comfort. She was beginning to think that their unexpected visitor was a very nice individual. He seemed to really appreciate what they were doing for him and he seemed eager to help out any way that he could.

Bud laid down on the sofa in the pool room and thanked Irene again for her help. He lay there for a while just thinking about himself and his predicament. It certainly seemed that somebody, or somebodies had tried to do him serious harm, but, like some old alley cat, he'd landed on his feet. Maybe a little shaken, a little broken, but he would heal up and go on living. He couldn't help wondering what the judge would find out about him. He knew it would be some time before they had any information. He tried to think of what relatives he might have. He knew he wasn't married and that he didn't have any children. He couldn't remember having a girlfriend, but he wished he did. Having someone to love makes tough times a lot easier. But, all in all, he

18

was alive and in pretty good shape except for his ankle and his head, but how long would it take for his memory to come back. Finally he could feel himself falling asleep, and it was a very comforting feeling.

Irene asked the boys to help her clean up while she washed the dishes. It occurred to her that one thing the man could help her with was running the store. The boys would be back in school in a few weeks and she would have much less time on her hands.

Dr. Barnes dropped by the next day to check on the stranger's progress. Bud was sitting at the big table in the store playing Fred's synthesizer.

"You found a keyboard to play, that's nice," he commented.

"Yeah, it belongs to Loretta's brother, he was nice enough to let me borrow it. On Saturday a bunch of people are coming over here to jam, it will give me something to set my mind to besides worrying."

"Ah, I'm sorry for your anxiety. It will just take time before you're feeling better." Doc replied.

Bud said, "You know, it's a funny thing, there can be something you're trying to think of, like the name of something. You try to think about it and you get nowhere. Then, you start thinking about something else, then BOOM, the name pops up in your head."

"That's right," Doc replied, "and it will probably be very much like that for you for a good while. What names have you remembered lately?"

"Oh, uh, licorice- I couldn't think of the name. I remembered the taste and the smell, then the name popped into my mind. And pepperoni, I knew what it looked like and what it tasted like, then the name popped into my head."

19

Doc said, "It's funny about odors. You smell something familiar, but you can't remember where you smelled it before. It's completely baffling. Then, later on, it comes to you- like the smell of your grandmother's kitchen, or the barber shop you used to go to when you were a kid. That happens to me all the time. You know, it might be a good thing to get yourself a notebook and write stuff down. Then you'll have a record of how and when the recovery process took place."

"I'll do that, that'll give me something else to do and it will remind me of the progress I'm making. Thanks Doc. I know I'm somebody, it's just that, for the time being, I'm among strangers, but it would be the same if any single person went to a strange place. And just because I'm a stranger to everybody here now, it won't stay that way, we'll all be friends."

Doc smiled, "You know, you have a very good outlook on things, that's why I think things will work out for you. I don't know if you're a Bible reading person. I'm no expert myself, but there's a passage in Exodus, about when Moses left Egypt. He was taken in by some people and he worked with them. Made himself useful, so to speak. He married a woman- she was named Zipporah, I think, and she bore him a son that he named Gershom, and said 'I was a stranger and in a strange land."

"I've heard that before. It seems a lot like my case. Not that I'm going to marry somebody, but heck, you never know." Bud replied.

"Well what time is that musicians meeting going to happen?" Doc asked, "I'd like to listen in on that."

"Around, three o'clock," Bud replied, "I'm not promising how good it will sound, just a bunch of amateurs."

"Well, you know where the word 'amateur' comes from don't you," said Doc.

"I guess not," said Bud.

"Amo is Latin for love," Doc explained, "It's what you do out of

20

pure love- with no expectation of reward."

"I think I've heard that before," Bud replied, "hey another one of those memory clicks."

"I think it's called 'déjà vu'" said Doc, "Well, I better get back home before it gets any later, but I'll try to be here on Saturday afternoon."

On Saturday morning Bud was up early making bread dough. Irene came in at about eight o'clock. "How many crusts are you going to make?" she asked Bud.

"That depends on how many you want me to make for today, and how many you want to freeze."

"Tough decision. Make, oh, about four for today and, I guess, I've got room for ten in the deep freeze. So fourteen."
"Sounds good," said Bud, I'll go ahead and let four rise and start topping them off around one, and start baking them at two."

"You're a man with a plan. Tell me, about how much do the ingredients cost to make a pizza?" Irene wanted to know.

"It seems like it comes out to around twenty-five cents per ingredient. So if you have dough, tomato paste, mushrooms, olives, onions, bell peppers, cheese, and pepperoni, that's, what, eight times a quarter, it's about two bucks a pizza."

Irene chuckled, "Not bad. I can see how the pizzerias make a pretty good profit. Would you mind showing my boys how you make it?"

"No problem, just send them in here, the more the merrier."

Chapter 3

Seven people showed up for the jam. There were two fiddlers-
Ace and Ruth. Dexter played guitar and also flute. Charles played
the bass. Maggie and Sarah played guitars and had good voices.
Kate played guitar and Fred played guitar and harmonica. Dr.
Barnes and his wife Ida were there. Most of the musicians brought
along a folding chair because there weren't enough chairs in the
store for everybody. Most of the music was country-western and
old popular songs.

Ace was a veteran fiddle player who had started at a very young
age. His favorite piece to play was a medley, starting with Liza
Jane and ending with Whiskey Afore Breakfast. Ruth hadn't been
playing as long as Ace, but she loved it and was learning more all
the time. Kate and Fred were primarily guitar players. Fred was
learning keyboard but he didn't mind Bud borrowing his
synthesizer, since he needed to relearn his chops. Fred and
Maggie were a couple who played a variety of old tunes. Dexter
played half a dozen instruments, with a lot of skill. But the real
star was Sarah. She had been singing since she was a small child
and had a three octave range with a beautiful tonal quality. Doc
said later that it was worth the visit just to hear Sarah's voice.

Everybody remarked on the pizza. Kenny and Jimbo were both
excited about learning the whole process. Several people said it
was better than you could get in any restaurant.

It was around six o'clock when several people said they had to
go home and fix supper. A few of them stayed 'til six thirty or so.
Jim Tanner stayed behind to have a word with Bud. "Hey man, do
you think you could drive a deuce and a half truck?" he asked.

"I don't know, I guess I could," said Bud, "Why, you got
something going?"

22

"Well, about once a week I haul a load of chickens over to Pine Bluff, and bring back some supplies for these folks around here. But I also hang drywall for some contractors, and if I get a chance to work overtime and get time and a half, I'd need somebody to make the run for me. See, I own this truck and I make a lot of income with it."

Bud rubbed his chin, "I guess I could take a crack at it."

"Ok," Jim replied. "Well, I'll be making the run on Monday, why don't you ride along with me and see if you can handle it. Suppose I came around Monday morning and picked you up?"

"Ok, that'll work," Bud replied. They shook hands and Jim went home.

In the morning Kenny came in and asked Bud if he wanted to go to church. Bud declined. "See, I wouldn't mind going with you, but until we get it cleared up about whether I'm safe or not, I'd rather not meet a bunch of new people."

"Well, that's sort of what Mom thought," said Kenny said. "My next question is, do you know anything about plumbing?"

Bud shook his head and grinned, "People keep asking me these questions. Let me come look at what you need fixed. I'll try to figure out what to do." He followed Kenny out the door into the back yard. There was a pipe sticking up out of the ground with a faucet attached. Jimbo had been mowing the yard when the mower had kicked a rock into the pipe and caused a small leak. The water had been shut off at the main valve but there was nowhere else to shut it off.

"Aw, shucks," Bud commented, "I can handle that. Have you got an old inner-tube?"

"Got one for a bicycle, but it leaks."

"That'll work fine. Just leave it with me and I'll have it fixed before you get back."

The residents of Pine Valley, dressed in their best clothes, were piling into station wagons and pick-up trucks to head for their churches. Their styles of clothing were a little different than what you would see in a typical American suburban neighborhood. There were more bright reds; on both women and men, and the women's dresses were adorned with sequins and rhinestones. The men tended toward cowboy boots or two-tone loafers.

Bud searched around and found a package of sandpaper in the store. He used it on the area surrounding the leak in the pipe. He cut a long strip from the inner tube. Pressing one end of the strip over the hole in the pipe, he simultaneously stretched the rubber and kept it taut as he made eight wraps around the pipe. Then, he held it down again with his thumb while he slipped the loose end through and pulled it tight to hold the wrap in place. Then he cut off the loose end. It wasn't a permanent fix, but it would hold until he could get the necessary parts to repair it permanently. Then he began to wonder how he knew how to do what he had just done. He must have done it before, but he couldn't conjure up the memory of when and where. Then he went and peered into the crawl space, looking for the shut-off valve. He quickly came to the conclusion that it would be better to wait until the family returned from church rather than spend a lot of time crawling in the dirt.

The afternoon was spent fixing "dinner." Loretta and her family came over to the store and brought food with them to share. "What kind of greens are these?" Bud wanted to know.

"Mustard," Loretta told him.

"Didn't know you could eat mustard greens," said Bud, "they're pretty good."

"You've got to be a northern boy," said Irene. "Hey, nice job you did on the yard faucet. How'd you learn to fix a leak that way?"

"That's the funny thing, I don't know." Bud replied.

24

A little later the phone rang. Jimbo answered it. "Pine Valley Store. Oh, hi Doc, yeah he's right here." He handed the phone to Bud.

Doc said, "I need to look at that ankle, what are you doing in the morning?"

"Jim Tanner's coming in the morning and we're driving to Pine..."

"Bluff?"

"Yeah, that's it."

"Well go easy walking on that foot and come see me when you get back."

"Ok, Doc, I will." Bud replied, "See you later."

Later that night, after Bud had gone to bed, he lay on his back and thought about the events of the day. He had fixed a pipe with an old inner-tube. He could play a piano. These people in Pine Valley were treating him real well, even though they had met just a few days ago. Jim was coming tomorrow so he could ride with him to Pine Bluff. Doc wanted to see him when he got back. He had a feeling he could drive that truck, even though he couldn't remember doing it before.

The next morning, Jim Tanner was the first to enter the store. He arrived at seven and Bud was dressed and waiting. They both had a piece of Irene's pie and a cup of strong coffee. Bud mused over the fact that the persimmons and he had arrived in Pine Valley the same day. Just as they were about to leave, the phone rang and Irene answered. It was for Bud.

"Hello, Bud, this is Albert James, your attorney."

"Oh, hello Judge, what have you got?" Bud asked.

"I've spoken with the state attorney general about your case. I had a suspicion from the outset that you might be the victim of a witness-protection program turned bad. When I described your case to him he agreed that it was a good possibility. He's going to contact the federal boys when he has a chance and try to figure out what the score is. Of course, we're keeping this all on the cue tee, so we don't put you at risk. You're safe here with us and we'll keep it that way if you understand what I mean."

"I do, your honor, and I really appreciate your help. I'm going with this guy named Jim Tanner to Pine Bluff to find out how to run this route for him if he needs me," said Bud.

"Oh yeah, I know Jim, he's a good man. Well, you go ahead and do your run. I don't know how long it will take the AG to get his information, but I'll be in touch with you as soon as he calls me. Have a good trip," the judge replied.

"Thanks, your honor, and thanks for calling."

Jim and Bud started off for the run to the chicken plant. They didn't talk much for the first twenty miles. Bud observed the way Jim was driving the truck. Then he said, "Must be a two and a half."

"Yeah, that's right," Jim replied, "ever drive on of these?"

"I think I have. Two speed rear axle?"

"You've driven one a lot?"

Bud didn't answer right away. He thought for a minute. Then he said, "I think I might have owned a truck like this."

"Well I'll be damned," said Jim, "You're just the man I need."

"Let me get this ankle healed up and I'll be ready to go."

"Well, all right. Let's stop in Prescott and get a cup of coffee, I know a good place," said Jim.

Over coffee Bud tried to give Jim some idea of the strange reality in which he found himself. It was like having a box full of important documents, but the box was locked and he had lost the key.

"But the good thing is, things will come back to me in time."

26

Jim nodded, "I can understand that. It's funny, you know, lots of folks are trying to forget things and others are trying to remember. Ever been to Pine Bluff? Oh hell, I guess you don't know. There's more black folks there than any other place in the state."

Bud said, "I don't know exactly, but as well as I can remember, most black folks have treated me as well as any white folks."

"I've kind of had the same experience. Most of the folks working at the poultry processing plant are black. They don't make a lot of money, but it's a regular job and most of them are just trying to get by. Just about the whole state depends on the chicken industry," Jim related. "Oh well, let's get back on the road. Hit the rest room if you need to."

When they were on the road again Bud asked Jim about the working environment at the poultry plant.

"Well, it's like this, the biggest problem is slipping and falling. The floor gets greasy and it's easy to slip and fall and hurt yourself. Broken elbows, broken collar bones, broken wrists- that kind of thing."

"Why collar bones?"

"If you land on your shoulder hard enough, the strain is all on your collar bone."

"What can they do about it?" Bud wanted to know.

"They've got hot-water hoses and detergent to wash off the grease. Trouble is, while they're doing that, they have to turn off the conveyor belts, and the time they spend doing that, the company's not making money. OSHA has a time schedule set up for degreasing, but the supervisors get to decide when to stop. Well, their attitude is, 'You're covered by workman's comp,' but, that's not as good as not getting injured in the first place, and it

27

always comes down to, how often you degrease the floor."

"I can relate to that," said Bud. "They want the workers to cooperate with them when they don't have the best interest of the workers in mind. They want them to compete among themselves but cooperate with management."

"Exactly," said Jim. "The workers should be able to say, 'hey, you want cooperation, let us wash down the damn floor when it gets greasy, is that asking too much?'"

"Right," said Bud, "If it was their ass hitting the floor they'd feel a lot different about it." They both started laughing. "Does the interstate take us to Pine Bluff?"

"No we have to get off up here a ways and head to Sheridan." Jim replied.

"Wasn't Sheridan a Union General?"

"Yeah, they named the county Grant and the town Sheridan because it was supposed to be a place for northern people to settle. I guess a few of them did, but it's hard to find anybody in Grant County who descended from Yankees. It's the same with Union County and Lincoln County, over south and west of here. The folks aren't a bit different than they are in the other seventy-two counties. Anyway, we go east on two-seventy 'til we get to White Hall, then we get onto I-five-thirty, which takes us to Pine Bluff."

"I see, but weren't there any northern people that, more-or-less, stood out in the community?"

"Oh yeah, there was Col. Sam Fordyce. He was from Ohio. He figured the war wouldn't last too long so he tried to make it so not so many people would get killed. It was all a question of getting the South to lay down their arms. Then, when the war was over, he moved to Hot Springs so he could lay in the hot water and get over his injuries."

28

"That's amazing, what else did he do?"

"Well, first he built hotels and bathhouses, then he started building railroads. Built most of the railroads in Arkansas."

"That's just amazing. How come I didn't learn about him in history class?"

"You didn't take Arkansas history."

"Well, no, but a guy like that you should hear more about."

"I guess they just teach us about the generals. Once you get down in ranks to the colonels and majors, they're not important enough."

"I guess not."

They stopped in Sheridan for lunch. "Order whatever you want," Jim told Bud.

"A buck seventy-five for a BLT?" Bud mused, "I feel like I've gone back in the past."

"And they serve you fast here, save a little time, don't lose any chickens."

"I saw a sign back there said 'Mad Butcher', I don't know if I'd want to meet a crazy guy with a meat cleaver in his hand." Bud remarked.

Jim laughed, "I've wondered that myself, but he's been in business for a long time."

Lunch over, they headed for White Hall. Bud had noticed there wasn't much traffic since they had left Pine Valley, but by the time they turned onto I-five-thirty, there were a few more trucks on the road. The chicken plant took up almost an acre and the parking lot was just as big. Most of the cars and pick-up trucks were at least ten years old. The loading dock was on one end of the building. Bud got out of the cab before Jim backed up to the loading dock. Jim told him he didn't need to do anything, but Bud was a guy who couldn't sit around when things were happening.

29

He helped Jim hand the chicken cages to the plant people until he felt pressure on his injured foot. Then he sat down on a crate to rest for a while. Nearly all of the plant employees were African-American. Bud introduced himself to a few of them, and told them he would be driving this route in the near future. Later on he asked Jim what the people earned at the plant.

"Whatever federal minimum wage is." Jim replied. "Since prices of most stuff here is pretty reasonable, they're not having a hard time getting by. Like I said, it's working on that slick floor that's their biggest worry."

"So, are there signs up telling them what the safety regulations are?" Bud wondered.

"Yeah, they have signs. But some people can't read. A while back it came to the attention of OSHA that some folks couldn't read the signs. So they passed a new regulation that management was to make sure the signs were read to everybody, and if a new sign goes up, they're supposed to tell everybody what it says. There's a law that whenever an accident happens, OSHA has to know about it. If there's an injury, the company can be fined. If there's an accident and OSHA isn't informed, there's a big whopping fine, so big the company doesn't want to risk it."

"Sounds like the people are pretty well protected." Bud commented.

"They should be, but the problem is, unless you have a few people around who make it their personal goal to keep OSHA informed, people can have accidents and can get conned into not reporting it. If there was a union, it would be the steward's job to take care of all that, but every time there's a vote for a union, they always vote it down. The company manages to make them believe that if they go union they'll lose their jobs. They could lose their jobs, but that wouldn't be the reason for it."

The loading finished, one of the plant employees, a woman they called Big Sally asked them if they would like a chicken sandwich.

Bud said, "I appreciate the offer, but the odor of this place- no offense intended- kind of spoils my appetite."

The woman chuckled, "Oh no offense taken, we're here all the time and we never even notice the smell. I'll put the chicken and bread in a bag and you can take it along. By the time y'all are on your way, your appetite will come back."

"Well, all right, thanks." Bud replied.

The 'sandwich' was a large fried chicken breast with two pieces of white bread. Along with everything else, the plant produced frozen, breaded chicken parts and the employees kept an electric deep-fryer on hand for when anyone wanted a snack. Jim Tanner remarked how it was one of the unwritten benefits of working in a place that produced food. The thought that crossed Bud's mind was that he must have had pizza handy wherever the pizzeria was where he'd learned his cooking skill.

It was approaching five-thirty when Jim and Bud arrived back in Pine Valley. Kenny and Jimbo were anxious to know what Bud's day was like. The thought crossed Bud's mind that the boys had a certain interest in him because of their lack of a role model. He had a nagging feeling that this wasn't the first time in his life that he was in that type of a situation, but he couldn't quite put his finger on just where or when he had had that same feeling. "Yeah, it's a good ways over there to Pine Bluff," he told the boys, "but it's an easy drive. I'm ready to make that run for Jim whenever he needs me. Seems like a lot of places around here have 'pine' in their name. Isn't there a song about piney woods?"

"Irene said, "Yes, there's a Buffy St. Marie song called 'The Piney Wood Hills', it's about some place in Canada, but there are a lot of places that have piney woods. Besides here there's Louisiana, the Appalachian Mountains, the Rocky Mountains- they're all over. By the way, Dr. Barnes wants you to call."

"Oh, thanks. It's not long distance is it?"

"No, you can use the phone at the cash register."

"Hi, Doc, this is Bud, you wanted me to call?"

"Yes, I need to take a look at that foot and see how you're coming along. And, the judge has been talking to the attorney general and he has information and needs to talk with you. Are you busy tomorrow?"

"No, Doc, I'm not doing anything special."

"Why don't I come by and pick you up after breakfast, and we'll go over and talk to Judge James."

"That's fine with me, I'll see you tomorrow then, and thanks for your help." Bud hung up the phone and went back to talk to Irene.

"Well, how was your day, Bud?" she asked.

"Well, like I was telling the boys. This place is a lot less urban than where I've been before. Even though I don't remember much about it, I'm pretty sure there were a lot more people, and more concrete, and lots of cars making a lot of traffic."

"Yeah, it's pretty rural here, but Texarkana is about thirty-five miles away, and Little Rock is a hundred miles the other direction."

"I just kind of remember that outside of town it was all suburban."

32

"Yeah, I think I know places like that. I think it takes a population of about a hundred thousand or more to be like that. Anyway, your memory seems to be coming back. We're all glad to see that."

"Yeah," said Jimbo, "Pretty soon you'll know where you came from."

"And who your relatives are." said Kenny.

Bud said, "Of course there's always good memories and bad memories. I'm just hoping that the good outweighs the bad."

Bud played crazy eights with Jimbo and Kenny until ten o'clock, then he laid down on the couch in the pool room and tried to sleep. He slept fitfully the whole night. When he woke he had been dreaming about a chrome horse. It reminded him of a song by Bob Dylan. Irene had whipped up some waffles and patty sausage. The boys were at the table enjoying theirs when he emerged from the pool room. "Do you like waffles, Bud?" Irene asked.

"If that's what these things are, they're my favorite. Yesterday I found out I love fried chicken. Now I know I love waffles too. Pass the syrup. Oh lord this smells good."

Irene poured him a cup of coffee. "So you're going to see Doc this morning?" she asked.

"Yes, and Judge James too. I'm expecting them to have some information for me. I hope it isn't the shocking kind of information."

Irene said, "Just enjoy your breakfast and try not to worry about it."

"That's very good advice, Irene, I'm going to try to do just that. Tell me, was there a Dylan song about a chrome horse?"

33

"Hmm, yeah, let me think. 'You ride on your chrome horse with your diplomat, who carries on his shoulder a Siamese cat...' I think it's 'Like a Rolling Stone."

"Yeah? Well, I woke up this morning from dreaming of a chrome horse. But it wasn't a song- it just reminded me of a song. It was a horse made out of pieces of chrome bumpers- all welded together."

"It must mean something, Bud." Irene commented.

"Yeah, just another one of those 'clicks'." Bud replied.

Chapter 4

When Doc arrived, Judge James was in the car with him. "Let's go over to my place," Doc suggested.

As they pulled onto the road Bud said, "Can I make a request?" "Sure," said the judge, "What'll it be?"

"Could you guys start talking, please- the anxiety is killing me."

"Oh sure," said the judge, "I fully understand. Well I'll start by saying the attorney general heard back from the FBI. They're pretty sure they know who you are."

Bud said, "Aaaaaah, that's a relief. And…"

"I'm sure you needed that. And, we're dealing with bureaucracy here, you know, red tape. But they believe you're in no imminent danger here. You were, in fact, in witness protection. They have, or will have, notified some people that you would have been connected with, when you had been relocated. Namely, your employer and your landlord, so they'll know they don't have to worry about you. Can we wait until we get where we're going? I've got some stuff I need to read to you." Judge James concluded.

"Oh sure, whew, you don't know how relieved I am to hear that much." Bud sighed.

When they arrived at the doctor's house, Mrs. Barnes met them at the door. "My dear," the doctor began, "this is our friend Bud that you've heard us speak about. The three of us need to have some privacy so we can discuss things."

"Nice to meet you, Bud," she said, "I saw you over at the store on Saturday, but we didn't get introduced."

"Nice to meet you," Bud replied. Dr. Barnes motioned the other two men towards a large couch and he sat in an armchair.

"Now let me look here," the judge began. "Have there been any recent recollections you've had, Bud?"

"Not a lot, sir. I think at one time I owned a truck like Jim

Tanner's. A two and a half ton box-bed. Also, I had a dream about a horse made out of chrome." They sat silent for a moment.

Then the judge said: "That's very interesting. If you're the person they think you are, you were driving a delivery truck that fits the description of the truck you mentioned." Judge James paused for a minute, then he said, "Also, if I'm not mistaken, the place you were working, Wichita, Kansas, has a sculpture, on a downtown sidewalk, of a horse made out of pieces of chrome bumpers, welded together."

"Yeah, that's what it looked like," Bud interjected.

"Ah," said the judge, "it can't be just coincidence. Now let me explain something. The federal boys are assuming that you're somebody they put in witness-protection, and what subsequently happened was an act of revenge perpetrated by whoever you testified against. That becomes another crime they committed. And they have an ongoing investigation of the person or persons involved. So they don't want anybody to know, first, that you're alive and well, and second, where you are and what you're doing. So, for the time being, they don't want anyone to know anything about their operation, and that includes you and us. They're going under the assumption that, where you are now, you're safer than where you were living."

Dr. Barnes said, "While you're thinking about that, let me have a look at that ankle."

"Oh, sure," Bud replied, "and I do need to think this over for a minute."

Bud raised his foot onto an ottoman and the doctor began unwrapping the bandage. Once the bandage was removed, the doctor pressed the skin down to check for edema. While he was doing this the judge continued. "The name you were going by in Kansas was Ray Collins. Does that ring a bell at all?"

"Yes, vaguely. What else can you tell me?"

"You had a job driving a delivery truck. The justice department had provided you with a little money, which you mostly used to buy a used Pontiac. The abductors apparently stole the car, but for some reason, abandoned it. The justice department doesn't want you to go back there and suggests that you just forget about that whole arrangement."

"Well, I've already done that," Bud said with a chuckle. Dr. Barnes and Judge James both laughed. "Well, what can you tell me about before that?"

Judge James said, "Just briefly, you were working in south Texas. That's where you got on the wrong side of somebody and wound up testifying about them."

"Well, like they say, it must have seemed like a good idea at the time." The two other men laughed again. "So, is that all you can tell me?"

"The name they knew you by there was Colin Rayburn." The judge let Bud mull that over for a moment. "And that's pretty much it," said the judge, "The only other thing is that they're going to provide you with a new identity and twenty-five hundred dollars. It will come to me in the mail in about a week. How does that sound?"

"Actually it sounds pretty good. If it's all the same to you guys, I think I'll just keep being 'Bud.'"

"Fine with me," said the judge. The doctor also agreed.

Dr. Barnes was manipulating Bud's ankle in order to determine if he had any persisting joint problem. "You have a lot of small bones in your ankle and they all have cartilage in between. If you're not having any sharp twinges when you move your foot around, I'd have to say the healing process is well on its way. I think, if you just keep in mind that you have to be easy on it for the time being, we can leave the bandages off."

"Trust me, I'll be careful. They tried to do me in, but I came out all right," was Bud's comment.

Judge James looked like he was about to say something, paused a moment then said, "You're still kind of a mystery man. We'll learn more about you as time goes on, I expect. We don't know about your education or what you've done. That's ok, you're here, and we like you. If I can help you in any way just call, ok?"

"Thank you, I will," said Bud.

Dr. Barnes said, "I guess I'll take you back over to the store. Mrs. Barnes has some chores for me to do."

When they arrived at the store, Bud said, "Thanks, Doc, I can't tell you how much I appreciate all you've done."

"It's ok, Bud, I understand how you feel. Listen, if you need to talk to me about anything, just call, all right?"

Bud stepped out of the car. "I'll do that Doc. Bye now."

Chapter 5

When Bud entered the store, Irene said she had a message for him.

"Arlene Amonette wants to talk to you. Her number is over there by the phone."

"Which one is Arlene," Bud asked.

"When y'all were jamming on Saturday, she was the tall gal with the sandy hair."

"The one who's as tall as me?" Irene nodded. "I wonder what she wants."

"You'll find out when you talk to her," Irene replied.

Arlene answered on the first ring. "Hi, Arlene, this is Bud, what's up?"

"Ah, well, I just happen to have tickets to go see Jimmie Dale Gilmore in Texarkana next weekend. Ever heard of him?"

"Gee, I don't know. Does he sound kind of like Willie Nelson, but he's younger?"

"That's a pretty good description," Arlene replied.

"It sounds like it would be fun, but I really don't have any clothes to wear. I've got some money coming in a week or so, but I'm hard up right now," said Bud.

"Well, hell, if you've got money coming, why don't I lend you my credit card and we can run over to Dequeen and get you some clothes," Arlene replied.

"Hmm, you really make it hard for a guy to say no." Bud glanced over at Irene, who was smiling. "Yeah, I guess so."

"Great," said Arlene, "what are you doing around four o'clock?"

"Oh, I'm not busy," Bud replied.

"Well, I'll come pick you up and we can go from there." said Arlene.

"All right, I'll be here. Yeah, I'll talk to you later." He looked at

Irene, "I guess I have a date. What do you think?"

"Well," Irene began, "She's a pretty good sized gal. It's not easy for a gal like her. She might have been waiting a long time for a single, tall guy to come around. You are single, aren't you?"

"Oh, I'm sure I am. They relocated me in Wichita and I was single then so I'm sure I still am." Bud confided. "You know, I hope I'm not, well, being presumptuous or something…"

Irene smiled, "You mean, about me? Nah, see there is a local guy who I've been seeing for quite some time. Have you ever watched Andy Griffith?"

"I think so, was he a sheriff?"

"Yeah, well you know how he had the same girlfriend for many years? Well that's the kind of relationship I'm in. One of these days he'll come to his senses and realize I'm not anything like his ex-wife who was just using him. But, no, just play it by ear. Men and women need each other. We really do."

Irene's boyfriend was named Billy Fred Driscoll. He was about fifty-five years old. He had a business on the highway outside Dequeen where he sold portable storage buildings and small trailers. The storage buildings could be moved easily with a modern tow-truck. For the business to function, it was necessary that someone was always there during daylight hours, six and a half days a week. Small town people were likely to come in looking for one of his units with no prior warning.

Arlene was as tall as Bud, but she was heavier built. Her face was attractive, if a person actually looked at her face. She hated it when a shorter person bumped into her and said, 'Oh, excuse me sir.' She had a Ford pick-up with a back seat. When she arrived at the store she parked in front and came inside. She smiled at Bud and held out her hand. "You made my day already, Bud."

"You made mine too," Bud replied as he took her hand. "Would you like a cup of coffee?"

40

"Nah, I'm as revved up as I can stand," said Arlene, "how do you feel about western clothes?"

"Well, it is country music, isn't it?" They climbed into her pick-up and headed east.

"There's a shirt they have at Walmart that I've always wanted to see on a guy, and I think you're that type of guy," Arlene allowed. "It's a light color and has a band across the chest and arms that has pictures of horses."

"I like horses," said Bud, "especially ol' Gordy who carried me out of the creek bottom a while back."

They pulled into the parking lot on Colin Raye drive. "Who's Colin Raye?" Bud wanted to know.

"He's a country singer who came from here. When you have a hit record around here, they name a street in your home town for you."

"That's interesting," Bud replied, "In a past life I was named 'Colin Rayburn', but keep that to yourself, I'm supposed to be in witness protection."

"Your secret's safe with me."

They looked all through the western shirts but there wasn't one like Arlene's choice that would fit Bud, but there was a darker shirt with a band of Native American motif that was his size. When Bud returned from the fitting room, Arlene said, "Perfect."

"Me, or the shirt?" Bud asked.

"Both," she said with a grin.

"I really am going to pay you back for this..." Bud began.

"Oh, don't worry about that, we're just getting started. Let's go look at the jeans." After they found some suitable jeans Arlene said, "How do you feel about boots?"

"Ok, I guess," Bud replied.

"We need to go to another place, this store doesn't carry the

41

good stuff." Close by was a place called Tractor Supply Co. Bud found a pair of boots he liked which were cowboy style, but good work boots that he could wear every day. Bud kept thinking that he should feel embarrassed having a woman buy clothes for him, but he didn't feel embarrassed, and he didn't know why. He wondered if the sales people would go home and tell their family about how they sold clothes to this guy, and the girl whipped out her credit card and paid for it. Maybe they thought it was the guy's birthday. Maybe the guy was somebody they found wandering around in the creek bottom and the girl decided to dress him up proper and take him to a concert. They'd believe it was his birthday before they'd believe that.

"I hope you don't mind coming over and having supper with me," Arlene ventured.

"Uh, no, if you'll let me help with the cooking," Bud replied.

"Ok, we'll both cook, it's a deal," said Arlene.

Over supper, Bud asked what her occupation was. "I'm an animal caretaker."

"Excuse my ignorance, but I don't know what that is."

"This three hundred acres we're on belongs to Albert James and John Whitehall. This is a cow-calf operation and it's my job to see that these cows stay in good health. Each one is worth about five hundred dollars and you try to keep them alive. 'Animal caretaker' is what goes down on my income tax return. But it's fifty thousand bucks worth of livestock."

"I see," said Bud. "I wouldn't think there would be very many female animal caretakers."

"For a cow-calf operation, no. You should see some of the looks I get when I tell them what I do. Sometimes they laugh, but when I tell them how long I've kept a hundred head of cows without losing a single one they shut up." Arlene explained. "And I get this house rent-free, so it's a pretty good deal for a girl who loves to take care of animals. What do you think about macaroni and cheese?"

"Sounds good to me." Bud replied. He followed her into the small kitchen of the house.

Arlene opened the door to her refrigerator. "Oh no, this cheese has mold growing on it."

"Let me see that cheese," said Bud, "Oh, it'll be fine, let me cut the mold off and grate it for you." Arlene handed him the cheese and a knife. He trimmed off the moldy cheese, then grated it onto a small plate. "Believe me, if pizzerias tossed out the cheese whenever it got mold on it they wouldn't be making any profit."

The supper was simple, but it was tasty and it was filling. Bud had a feeling of being appreciated as a person. It was a welcome feeling. Welcome was just what Arlene had in mind. It was the fastest she had ever gotten close to another person that she could remember.

43

Chapter 6

In Wichita Ray hadn't shown up for work, and when his boss, Mr. Mc Grady, called his number there was no answer. Then he called Ray's landlady, Mrs. Mabry. She told him that Ray wasn't there and his car wasn't there either. Mc Grady thanked her and asked her to tell Ray to call him when she saw him.

At around five in the afternoon Bobby Dumford came looking for Ray. Bobby was tall for a sixteen-year-old. He lived with his grandmother, Mrs. Graves. When he didn't find Ray, he went to ask Mrs. Mabry if she knew where he was. "I don't know, Bobby, I haven't seen him since yesterday morning. He didn't show up at work and when I looked, his car was gone, that's all I know. It's not like him to not come to work and not to call. If I hear anything I'll call you."

Bobby felt a little unnerved. He had lost his father in a car wreck a few years ago and his mother had remarried. He lived with his grandmother because he felt comfortable with her. Ray Collins was a father figure to him. Ray was also good at math and helped him with his homework when school was in session.

Two days later he got a call from Mrs. Mabry. She told him that Ray's car was back but there was still no sign of its owner. She had called the Wichita police about it. Bobby knew the police would be there soon to tow the car away and he wanted to take a look at it before they got there. It was two blocks down and across the street and he hurried over. He knew they might be looking for fingerprints so he had to be careful about that. There were splotches of red clay on the lower part of the car. The keys were in the ignition. He couldn't see anything inside the car aside from a few scraps of paper. He looked in the trunk. It was dusty inside and there was a torn, blue plaid, short-sleeved shirt and a dirty sock. He left it in place and closed the trunk. He opened the passenger side door. There were a couple of cigarette butts on the floor. He found a wadded up slip of paper. It was a credit card receipt from a gas station in Ardmore, Oklahoma. He memorized the date and address and left the slip on the floor. On the driver's side he found another credit card receipt from Ardmore, Oklahoma. The date was a day later. He left it where he found it. He was sitting on the curb when the city police arrived. They asked him if he knew the car's owner.

"He was a friend of mine. He came here about eight months ago. He lived alone and I don't know much about him."

The officer asked him about places he might have hung out. "The only place I know of was at Town East. He used to go over there on weekends and play a synthesizer in front of a music store." He gave the officer his phone number and asked if they would call him if they found out anything. They told him they would.

Bobby's grandmother had sent him to the store for bread, milk, and eggs. He had been riding a twenty-six inch bike since he was twelve. He let himself into the back door of the house and put the sack on the kitchen counter. Then he heard his grandmother call. "Bobby, I need to tell you something," she said as she walked into the kitchen. "Mrs. Mabry needs to talk to you. She said for you to come on over when you get a chance. I think it's something to do with Ray Collins."

"Oh, thanks Mama, I'll go over there now if it's ok with you."

"That's fine with me," she replied.

Mrs. Mabry had been Ray's landlady when he disappeared about a few days earlier. Bobby went out the front door of his grandmother's house and crossed the street. She only lived a block away. Mrs. Mabry opened the door when he rang. "Come in, Bobby, would you like a glass of iced tea?"

"Sure," he answered.

45

"Sit down, I'll be right back." Bobby felt a little on edge. For the last few days he'd worried about his friend, fearing the worst. Mrs. Mabry soon returned and handed him a glass of tea. "Relax, Bobby, he's ok."

"Ah, that's good to hear," Bobby exhaled, "What happened to him?"

"Ok, what I'm about to tell you has to stay in strict confidence." Bobby nodded. "Ray was in a witness-protection program. That means he testified in criminal court to get somebody convicted of a crime. Well, they relocated him here in Wichita from two states away where they thought he was safe. But he wasn't. Somehow they found out anyway. These people kidnapped him and took him away in his own car. The FBI couldn't tell me where he is, but he's safe where he is and they want him to stay there and he's in no danger as far as they know. He had some minor injuries but he's healed up from those now." She paused for a moment. "The FBI came and took his car and they don't want anybody to even know he was here."

"So, that means I can't talk to him?"

"Not for the time being. I know he's a good friend of yours, that's why I wanted you to know. They're waiting to see how things go. Perhaps in the near future we'll hear from him, but for now he's better off than he was here. The only people who know are his boss that he worked for here, and you and me. And we can't tell anyone."

Bobby had relaxed a little by then. "I'm so glad to know he's ok. I've been losing sleep ever since he disappeared. Is it ok if I tell Mama?"

"You can tell her, but don't tell anyone else, and make sure she understands that it has to stay in strict confidence," said Mrs. Mabry.

"Oh, I understand, nobody needs to know. Well, I've got to get home, but thanks so much for letting me know. You don't know how relieved I am to not have to worry."

Bobby's grandmother, Mrs. Graves, was the person closest to him. With the death of her husband and other deaths in the family, she had the option of staying in the old family home and she was glad that Bobby was willing to stay there as well, since they could help each other. She was waiting at the door when she saw Bobby coming and she opened it as soon as he got there.

"It's ok, Mama. They found Ray and he's in a safe place. I guess he got on the wrong side of some criminal types."

"Oh, thank God," she said as she hugged Bobby. She was fighting back tears while he related to her that Ray was in good health and he was safe where he was. "Will we be able to get in touch with him?"

"No, Mama. Sometime he might get in touch with us. But we can't talk about this with anyone. He might be in danger if we did."

"Well, at least we know that he's safe and well. I know how much of a friend he was to you," she replied.

"There's one thing though," Bobby said, "the mobsters, when they kidnapped Ray, they carried him off in his own car. Then they brought Ray's car back and left it outside his apartment. The police came and got his car. That's what happened to it."

"What does that mean to us?" she asked.

"Well, I went through that whole car before they took it away, and I found two receipts from a station where they stopped for gas and paid for it with Ray's credit card. The place was in Ardmore, Oklahoma. One time they got twenty-four gallons, the other time they got twenty-three. So they must have gone far enough from Ardmore to use up a tank of gas."

"Oh dear, Bobby, if the FBI are handling this maybe we'd be

better off not getting involved."

"I know Mama, all we can do is hope they get it right. But, on the other hand, they brought him here, thinking he would be safe, and he wasn't. But I have an idea."

"What idea is that?" she asked.

"We could go down to Oklahoma where they were and look around."

"Oh, I don't know. I think it would be better to let the authorities deal with it. Oh, I know he means a lot to you. I'll have to think about it."

"Mama, they just went straight south on I-thirty-five and probably turned off onto US seventy."

"I'll have to think about it, ok?"

"Thanks Mama, I just think there's no harm in looking."

Chapter 7

Bud had spent the night with Arlene several times. She asked him if he felt comfortable about it. "You know there's one thing that has given me that feeling like I've been here before."

"Is it with respect to Irene?" she asked.

"No, Irene's got something going with another guy. But that's not what you were asking was it?"

"No, I just threw that in. What do you think about us?"

"I just think, I guess it makes me feel kind of secure. I can't bring myself to dwell on what all it might mean in the distant future because I can't remember big chunks of my past."

"Well, maybe in time it will all come back." She was trying to be assuring.

"Yeah, time. But how much?" he mused.

"As long as it takes, I guess," she replied.

Bud started to laugh, "That's it. As long as it takes."

"Well let me say this, as long as you want to be with me," she explained, "just know that I want to be with you. Does that make sense?"

"Yeah, I like the sound of that."

"So we can be a couple?" Bud didn't say anything, he just got up and took her hands in his. She stood up and they had a long embrace.

The phone rang. It was Judge James- he wanted to come over and talk to Bud. "It's the judge, do you want him to come over and talk?"

"Why not," said Bud, "tell him to come on over." She told the judge to come and hung up the phone. "Now the question is: do you want to know about my precarious condition?" he said.

"Oh, I don't mind unless there is something you don't want me to know about."

"Nope, not at all, it's all about keeping me out of harm's way while I'm adjusting to private life."

When the judge arrived Arlene invited him in. "Well I guess you all are shacked up together. So she's in on all this, Bud?" Judge James commented.

"That's the situation. What have you got for me, sir?"

"I've got, a birth certificate, and necessary IDs, as well as a cashier's check for you to get by on while you're getting adjusted. The name they gave you is 'Carl Russell."

Bud examined the paperwork, nodding his head, then smiled. "This should do the trick, Judge. But like I said earlier, these folks all know me as 'Bud', and I think I'll just leave it that way."

Judge James said: "That's fine as far as I'm concerned. Say, did you ever hear about the conversation I had with John Whitehall when we first bought this place?"

Arlene laughed, "I kind of gave him some information about that."

Albert James continued, "Arlene was the caretaker here, and John wanted to get rid of her and find a male who could do a better job. I told him we could easily find a man who'd take the job, but not one who could do it better than Arlene, and if he didn't like that I could find myself another partner. 'Oh, no,' he says, 'if you think she's ok, that's fine with me."

"Just equal rights for women," was Bud's comment.

The judge was just about to walk out the door when he noticed something strange. A skunk was walking across the cow pasture. Normally skunks are nocturnal. "Arlene, have you got a shotgun?"

"Yes, what's wrong?"

"I think we've got a rabid skunk on our hands," said the judge. "I'll keep an eye on him while you load up." Arlene got her shotgun out of the closet and loaded two number four shells into the breach.

"Ok," she said, "where is he?" Bud and the judge were outside the door.

"I've lost track of him now."

"He's behind that little bush," Bud said. "You'll have to circle around so you don't fire into the cows. Oh, no, he's headed right for the herd." Arlene trotted toward a tree, just a few yards from the house. "Try a shot at him." Arlene quickly fired and the skunk went down. They trotted over to where he was lying.

Arlene exhaled and said, "You know what we have to do now?"

"What's that," Bud inquired.

"Take a close look at every single cow," she replied. "Those critters get totally aggressive and attack anything that moves."

Judge James said: "Well, besides that we've got to take this critter to get tested."

"How do we do that," Bud wanted to know.

Arlene replied: "Take him to a vet, who'll cut off his head and send it to the health department in Little Rock."

"How much does that cost?" Bud asked.

"That's all done for free," the judge replied. "If it cost anything nobody would do it. We used to have a problem with stray dogs pestering the cattle, but now, if anybody has a reason to shoot a dog, as long as the head gets sent to the health department, they're well within their rights."

"Now, we've got two reasons to go to Dequeen," Arlene allowed. Albert James said goodbye and headed home. Arlene and Bud put the skunk into a plastic bag in the back of her pick-up. When they got to town they went to the vet's office first. Dr. Hodges was none too happy to see what their gift was but he accepted it into his custody.

When they left the vet's office Bud asked Arlene if it was unusual for skunks to be rabid. "No, as a matter of fact it's all too common. In a year's time we'll have a handful of dogs and cats, and a few

51

horses and cows. All the rest are bats and skunks. And only striped skunks at that. The common scenario is that somebody with a bunch of hunting dogs in a pen suddenly hears the dogs all barking. A skunk, in broad daylight, crawls into the dog pen and attacks the dogs. The skunk gets killed by the dogs, but not before several of them get bitten. They usually haven't been vaccinated, so the owners have to get a vet to give shots to all the dogs and then keep them quarantined in the pen for several months."

"How many animals get bitten by bats?" Bud inquired.

"Oh, there aren't near as many bats as skunks. But if a human gets bitten, it's more often a bat. There was one occasion where a guy who died in the hospital had been bitten by a bat. He happened to be an organ donor, and they were in such a hurry to transplant his organs that they did four transplants before they found out that the guy died of rabies."

"Are you serious?"

"Unfortunately I am."

There were only a handful of people at the county clerk's office so it didn't take long to get Bud's driver's license. When they had that taken care of they went back to Arlene's place so they could examine the cows for possible bites. It took over two hours to check the cow herd. There was no evidence of any of them having been bitten. After giving it a lot of thought, Arlene and the owners decided to vaccinate the whole herd, and they kept a close eye on them for the next month or so.

The Jimmie Dale Gilmore concert in Texarkana was a pleasant experience for Bud. He realized that having a person with you that you cared about made all the difference in enjoying yourself. He also realized something else, which he mentioned to Arlene. "I just thought of something I'd lost sight of."

"What's that?" she wanted to know.

"Well, it occurs to me, I'm supposed to be keeping a low profile," he responded, "this kind of an event puts you in view of a lot of strangers."

"I guess you're right," she said, "but, on the other hand, if you aren't out around other people, life could get to be pretty constraining."

"Yeah, you're right, I guess it's just something that has its necessary benefits and non-benefits," he concluded. "You wouldn't want to be hiding out all the time."

Albert James was at home watching the TV news when the phone rang. It was Mr. Rogers, the state AG. "Albert, I've got somebody here that wants to talk to you, FBI agent Bishop."

"Yes, Mr. Bishop, what can I do for you?"

"Judge, I'm the only person currently working on that South Texas mob. I understand you're in touch with this fellow, Carl Russell," said agent Bishop.

"Yes, I am, but the only name he answers to is 'Bud'."

"Heh, heh, I can understand that. Can you give me some idea of his living situation?"

"Well, ok, he's got a job, he's got a girlfriend, has some other friends.
And he's met some other musicians he jams with."

"He plays music?"

"Yeah, you didn't know? He plays piano."

"I'll make a note of that. You see, we tried real hard to get him in a safe environment, but somehow they found him. As far as I'm concerned they added attempted murder to their case. I won't keep you, but I'd like to get a chance to talk him sometime."

"Well, sir, let me think about setting that up sometime in the near future. I'll get back with you about that."

"That sounds good, I'll be waiting to hear from you. Thank you, goodbye."

After he hung up the phone he asked his wife, "Lindy, what would you think about going up to the lake for an afternoon and taking Bud and Arlene along? We could get that FBI agent to come along and he might have information that would help Bud."

"I wouldn't mind doing that," she replied.

Albert called Arlene's house. His idea was to get Bud and Arlene and agent Bishop to go with him to Lake Ouachita. He had a cabin cruiser on the lake which was large enough for a dozen people. Bud and the agent could hang out by the dock and talk in privacy while the rest of them went fishing. Arlene answered the phone, "Howdy ma'am, here come the

judge." He explained his lake trip to her. She asked Bud, and it was fine with him. She decided to stay home and keep an eye on the herd. Bud asked if the Webb boys could go along. Judge James told him that was probably a good plan, he welcomed the chance to visit with the boys himself.

Chapter 8

Mrs. Graves was trying to get Bobby to make a plan they could follow in the process of looking for Ray Collins. "He won't be going by that name, Mama," Bobby told her.

"I know that, and it wasn't his real name anyway, but we know he's safe where he is." She paused for a moment. "Are we sure we won't be putting him in danger by doing this?"

"We can't be putting him in danger unless somebody's following us, and why would they do that since they stole his car and carried him off in the first place," Bobby replied.

"Ok, that makes sense," she said, "It helps me to be talking about these things so I can get a better idea of what the plan is. So we're going down I-thirty-five, to where?"

"Ardmore, Oklahoma. That's where US seventy crosses the interstate," he told her.

"And that's where they got gas?"

"They got gas there twice. Once on the way down and once on the way back. That's as much as we know. They brought the car back, probably because they wanted people to think he had just run off on his own. The car was rubbed clean of fingerprints. The only thing they overlooked was red mud on the tires and rims and two little crumpled-up pieces of paper."

Bobby worked as a bag boy at Dillon's. He asked his boss if he could have Friday off. His boss told him he'd rather him take Monday off, since Friday was a big day at the store. It sounded like a good idea, so he took Monday. He told his Grandmother about it and she said, "Let's leave Saturday morning, and if we get delayed or you get really tired, you'll be off on Monday."

Mrs. Graves' car was an eighty-three Chevrolet station wagon. It wasn't in primo condition, but it was reliable. Ray had showed Bobby how to change the oil and how to change the plugs and points, so Bobby wasn't worried about taking the car on a two hundred mile trip. They packed a suitcase apiece and Mrs. Graves made enough salami sandwiches to go there and back with a few to spare. They left early Saturday morning. The air conditioner didn't work so well but the weather wasn't too hot. Bobby let his grandmother take the first spell of driving.

"Have you looked at the map?" she asked.

"Don't need to, just head east on Kellogg and take I-thirty-five south. There'll be a sign that says Oklahoma City when we come to it," Bobby replied. The on-ramp was there just like Bobby said. There wasn't much traffic on the interstate but there were lots of trucks.

"Don't these trucking companies ever take a day off?" she asked Bobby.

"They'd be losing money all the time the trucks aren't moving down the road. They keep moving even when it's dark or the weather's bad. You might want to be on the outlook for pieces of tires coming off trucks."

"Tires don't come off of cars do they?" She commented.

"No, that's because they made recaps on cars illegal many years ago. But they're still legal on trucks- it's a way for them to save money," he told her.

"How can they do that if they're dangerous?" she wanted to know.

"There are high taxes on diesel fuel- that's what pays for the interstates. So they've got a lot of leverage with the lawmakers. All we can do is avoid driving in that space just behind and a little to the side of trucks- their blind spot on the right and the same space on the left, and keep an eye out for flying pieces of tire tread."

"I'm glad you told me about that," she said.

As they crossed the border into Oklahoma, Mrs. Graves made the comment that there were far fewer oil rigs than there used to be. "There are a lot of people who say that we still have lots of oil, they're just holding onto it," said Bobby.

"It's not that," his grandmother replied, "the production costs are so high that they can't compete on the world market. The primary reason that central Oklahoma is so populated is because there was so much oil money. When they quit drilling and pumping everything stagnated."

"Why did Wichita's economy get so stagnant?" he wanted to know.

"Apparently, most of the planes we were selling were being sold to the oil industry. Of course, Kansas has oil too, but while these oil men were raking in all this money, they could afford to have a Cessna or a Beech to fly back and forth to all their wells and drilling sites. Wichita was a booming place in those days. There were people moving here from all over the country. But now, owning an airplane is an expensive luxury few people can afford. Back then they built Century Two, the Mid-America All Indian Center, cleaned up the riverfront- Wichita was a showcase, everybody had a good job."

They stopped at the Ponca City exit and got coffee from a convenience store. Mrs. Graves said, "How do you feel about driving?"

"Oh, I can drive if you need a rest," Bobby replied.

"What's so strange about this is that we don't know where we're going," she said, except that it's somewhere east or west of Ardmore."

"Yeah, I know," Bobby replied, "But there's just something about putting your feet on the ground, driving the car down the road." He paused for a moment, "If we didn't do it, I'd be sitting around going crazy because I wasn't doing anything. Does that make sense, Mama?"

"Yes it does, Bobby, it does make sense," she said.

When they reached Oklahoma City it seemed like the

metropolitan area went on forever. They munched on the salami sandwiches as they made their way down the freeway. Thankfully they didn't have to exit and could stay in the center of the freeway and not have to change lanes. The traffic was heavy and at times they had to slow nearly to a crawl. It was a relief when they finally got to the southern edge of the city and the traffic moved more steadily.

As they reached Ardmore, Bobby started looking for the exit to US seventy. The first exit they came to was US seventy west so Bobby took it.

"What do you think about stopping for a cold drink, Mama?" Bobby asked.

"Fine with me," she replied. Bobby pulled into a Phillips sixty-six station and went inside. He went to the cash register with two cans of Sprite.

"Is that all for you?" asked the woman behind the counter.

"I guess so," Bobby replied.

"Dollar fifteen. You going to Wichita Falls?"

"No, I'm really not sure where we're going. I'm looking for a friend that disappeared a couple of weeks ago. Has anyone come in here recently looking for licorice?"

"Not that I recall. Usually, people going to Wichita Falls come this way. There's not too much out there, otherwise." She handed Bobby his change. "Good luck finding your friend."

"Thanks, I'll need it" Bobby replied.

He handed his grandmother the soda as he got in the car. "The lady at the counter said most people who come this way are headed for Wichita Falls, Texas."

"What does that tell us?" she asked.

"I don't know, I guess we can just head this way and see what we come to." They drove west toward a town called Wilson. It looked like farmland. Bobby was trying to think why somebody who was going to abandon another person would have a particular place they'd use as a destination. Somehow he just had a gut feeling that they'd be looking for more seclusion. Wilson had a casino. It was named 'Black Gold Casino.' There were about a dozen vehicles parked in front of it. Part of the neon lights were out on the roof of the building, so it read: 'BLACK   INO.'

Mrs. Graves said, "There's another reason for people to come this way."

The next town on the highway was called Ringling. There was a place on the highway named 'Mud Creek BBQ'. Bobby stopped in front of the place and thought about that being an inappropriate name for an eating place. The town seemed to be mostly on the north side of the highway, so he drove in that direction. He stopped in front of a Quick Trip. "Why are you stopping here?" asked his grandmother.

"Going to talk to the cashier just like I did in Wilson," he returned. He went in and looked right away at the candy section. They only had one brand of licorice, called 'A-one'. He walked up to the man at the cash register. "Does a tall dark middle-aged man come in and buy licorice?"

The man grinned, "Nah, there's a few that buys licorice, but nobody like that description. You looking for the guy?"

"Yeah, he disappeared a couple weeks ago. I think he's somewhere in Oklahoma." Bobby explained.

"Oklahoma's a big place." the man told him.

"Why is this town called Ringling?" Bobby asked.

"John Ringling started building a railroad here. The 'Oklahoma, New Mexico and Pacific," the man replied. "Good luck finding your friend."

"I'm praying for help," Bobby replied.

"Any luck?" asked Mrs. Graves.

"No, but I'm not discouraged. I have this vague feeling that Ray's most likely east of here rather than west." said Bobby.

"You mean east of Ardmore." Bobby nodded. Mrs. Graves said, "If you want to look in that direction, that's fine with me. This area has a desolate feel to it."

"It's all right country," Bobby replied, "I just think Ray is someplace more secluded."

They didn't talk much as they headed back to Ardmore. Mrs. Graves said, "Maybe we should stop for gas again in Ardmore."

Bobby said, "No, we don't need to, there'll be plenty of places, to get gas."

The next town of any size was Madill. After that they came to a huge lake, which the highway crossed. "You know, if those guys were looking for a place to get rid of Ray, they could have just dumped him in this lake," Bobby mused

"That's true," his grandmother replied, "so maybe murder wasn't their intention. What lake is this?"

"It's Lake Texoma. The Red River is the boundary between Texas and Oklahoma and the Corps of Engineers dammed it up to create a lake. I guess because they wanted hydroelectric power and people love to fish."

"So, just for the sake of speculation, why would these abductors be more likely to stay on highway seventy than to take a side road since they probably didn't have a specific destination?" Mrs. Graves wondered.

"Well, for one thing, these individuals aren't terribly smart, and, of course, I'm supposing here, not being familiar with their surroundings, they might have been wanting to keep it simple, and stay on one road both out and back," said Bobby.

His grandmother replied, "You know, for one so young, you really are systematic in your thinking."

"Thanks, Mama, I appreciate the vote of confidence. We may not succeed in this quest, but at least we tried. I'm thinking," Bobby

60

said, "that Ray's Pontiac had a twenty-four gallon tank, and would get around fifteen miles to the gallon. If my math is right, they should have had a range of around three hundred fifty miles. That's about the distance from Ardmore to the Arkansas border and back."

"So where highway seventy crosses the border is our target of inquiry?" his grandmother asked.

"That's my assumption," said Bobby, "I just hope I'm right."

Chapter 9

"Mr. Bishop, it's nice to meet you," said Bud.

"Nice to meet you, too. You can call me Pete," the agent replied. "I've got questions to ask you. I realize you don't have a lot of answers, but I have to ask anyway. You might have questions for me. Where do you want to start?"

"Why don't I start," said Bud.

"Ok, shoot."

"Where was I before I got sent off to Kansas?"

"You were in east Texas near the Gulf Coast- Houston, Galveston, it's a heavily populated area."

"Ok, knowing that, it might spark some memories. So these people were like a gang of some kind?" Bud wanted to know.

"That's basically what it is," said Pete.

"You would think if you were going to be a criminal you wouldn't want a whole lot of people to be in on it. Like, keep it simple and not get found out." Bud suggested.

"Well, I guess people tend to do things together whether they're honest or they're crooks. It's something they teach us about in training, crooks can be very complicated in the way they do things just like anybody else." Pete explained.

"Ok, don't take this as an insult, but what are the chances that somebody in law enforcement, could have, either by accident or knowingly, spilled the beans about where I was?"

"Ah," Pete made a tight-lipped smile, "the answer to that is, anything is possible, either accidently or otherwise. Does that make sense?"

"Yeah, I was thinking it could be kind of like a guy cheating on his wife. He doesn't want her to know, but she finds out anyway"

"It could very well be just like that."

"Well, what was I doing in the Houston area, if you don't mind me asking?"

"We were hoping you could help us with that. Are you saying you don't remember any of that?"

Bud didn't say anything for a minute or two. "That's what I'm saying, I don't remember any of that." He paused again. "I think I get the picture. You need for me to remember more about that before you can go further with this process."

Bishop smiled and nodded, "That's what we're hoping for." After a short pause Bishop said, "Now, I believe, originally you were from Indiana. Does that ring a bell?"

"Yeah, that's where I grew up. I graduated from high school there. I went to IU for a while, but it didn't work out. Then I started driving trucks. But after that, I don't know. I just don't know."

"Well, maybe later it will come back. We can't go any faster if we don't know." Bishop answered. "Ah, but you were a delivery driver in Texas. That much we know."

"Oh, ok, I was driving trucks. Yeah, I was driving. Let me take some time and think about that, something's bound to come back. But since I've been here in Pine Valley I found out that I can play a keyboard. I also found out I can make pizza. Doesn't seem like a lot, but it might relate to something else that happened or to some people I might have known."

Pete said, "Right, that's what you need to do, is just think about anything that happened during that time. I gave you my phone number, you can leave a message any time. I'm the only agent working on this case and you are my main contact. You don't need to tell any other person about this case, just me. Anything that happened, any person or persons, I need to know. Ok?"

"I understand, I'll definitely let you know if anything comes back to me. Now," Bud concluded, "I hope they get back pretty soon, I think I'd like to try catching some bass."

Albert James was helping the Webb boys with their bass fishing. He had a collection of rods, reels, and lures that went back thirty years. He had bought a dozen minnows at the bait shop at the docks when he renewed his fishing license. As a member of the legal profession he felt like he had to be licensed if he expected others to be. At that time of the summer he had always had pretty good luck by dropping a minnow about ten feet down. Jimbo and Kenny had each caught a one, or one and a half pound bass. Kenny wanted to put a smaller hook on his line and asked the judge how to tie it on.

"Well, Kenny, bite on that monofilament and lay that hook in the tackle box."

"I've already done that, sir."

"Thread the line through the loop about three inches, then wrap the line twelve or fourteen times around the line above, then slip the end through above the loop and pull it tight."

"Why not thirteen wraps?"

"Thirteen would be a hangman's noose and it's illegal to make a hangman's noose in the state of Arkansas."

"Is that true?" asked Jimbo.

The judge said, "It's what my daddy told me and it wouldn't be respectful to call your old man a liar. Why do you want a smaller hook?"

"To catch a crappie."

"Only let out about four or five feet of line, and keep twitching it every ten seconds. Use the smallest minnow."

Bud and Pete were standing at the dock waving. Albert James started the engine and maneuvered the boat slowly towards them. When he finally got close, Kenny held out a long-handled net which Bud grabbed and pulled them next to the dock. Bud and Pete climbed into the boat. The judge moved out about forty feet from the dock and cut the engine. Suddenly Jimbo let out a yell.

"Big one," he shouted. His rod was bent in a U shape. He was

64

reeling in and keeping the line taut. Then he couldn't make any headway with the fish but it was still pulling. "The line's hung," he said.

Bud said, "Hold on, I'll get him." He pulled his shoes and pants off and dived over the side. About five feet down he saw the crappie. The line was wound around a rock. He caught hold of the mouth of the crappie and managed to free the line from the rocks. Then he swam to the surface holding the fish by its gills. A cheer went up from the group.

"He's a diver," said Kenny.

"It's probably illegal to fish that way," Bud told him. They all laughed.

The judge said, "It's illegal if you speared him or if you caught him with your bare hands. Since he was hooked it doesn't matter how he was landed."

"Do you get many fishing infractions in court?" Pete Bishop asked.

Judge James said, "No, we don't. Most people who get cited for fishing infractions just pay the ticket. There are more 'no valid license' cases than anything else. There was one case where a guy took his grandchildren fishing when he didn't have a license. He tried to explain that he wasn't fishing, just the kids were. I asked him if he had, in the process, touched any of the fishing equipment. He nodded. I said, 'next time get a license.'
But, when it comes right down to it, we don't get too many fishing infractions in court."

Mr. Bishop said, "You know, I kind of wish I was into that kind of law enforcement rather than the stuff I'm dealing with. It used to be that people had rifles or shotguns they hunted with. Now there's thousands of people out there with three-fifty-seven magnums and assault rifles- especially if they're professional criminals. And the ones I deal with are mostly professional."

Bud added, "I'm sure glad the ones I ran into just abducted me

65

instead of bumping me off. I really am."

"That might a clue," said the agent, "let me know if you think of anything."

"I'll do just that," Bud replied.

Mrs. James handed Bud a towel and he thanked her as he began drying himself off. "I think it's been a long time since I've been in the water," he said, "Pete, could you drive me back over to Arlene's place? There's something I want to ask you about."

"Sure, whenever you're ready," the agent replied. Bud started getting dressed and began thanking the judge and his wife for their hospitality.

The judge said, "I'll take the kids back to the store, Bud. You go ahead with Mr. Bishop, I have a feeling you all need to talk."

"Thanks your honor," said the agent, "I'll be in touch."

Bud said to Pete Bishop, "I don't understand, if they had me testify in court, how come they don't know more about me than they do?"

The agent replied, "Well it's like this, they picked you because you didn't have family or friends that would have been put at risk. But they didn't go into it any deeper than that. Their main concern was to get a conviction on a mob boss, and they didn't pay much attention to who you were. Does that make sense?"

"Yeah, I guess it does."

On their way back to Arlene's, Bud started saying that something clicked while they were on the boat. "My dad died when I was an early teenager. The last thing we did together was go fishing. My dad hooked a bass and it got hung up in some brush- just like what happened today except it was brush instead of rocks. I dived in after it, just like I did today. It was big- about four pounds. That's the last time I've been fishing and the last time I've been in the water. It all came back to me. Then I remembered about high school. I could never read very fast but I always made good grades in math. By the time I was a senior, I had several teachers who thought I should go to college and several who thought I shouldn't. Well, I started at I.U., but I didn't do well in anything but math. So I decided that if I was to get a job and keep on reading regularly, I could improve my language skills. Did you ever have somebody tell you, 'there's no reason to misspell a word when you can look it up in the dictionary'? How can you look it up if you can't spell it?"

Bishop laughed, "Yeah, I know exactly what you mean. But what happens, if you manage to make it, and get a job in an office, you've got office people who can type, they can spell- you hand them a piece of paper that you jotted down on it what you wanted- they can give you back a beautiful letter."

"Well, that's something to think about," said Bud. "But what happened later, when my old man died, he left me some money. Not a lot, but a thousand or so. I bought a two and a half ton truck and I just started hauling stuff for people. I had a business card that read, 'need it hauled? Call Colin Rayburn.' I wasn't getting rich, but I was making a living."

"What happened to your mother?" asked Bishop.

"She was gone before that. I know she died but I don't remember how," Bud replied, "I guess that's all I can remember so far."

Pete Bishop was listening carefully, "What I really need to know about was what happened after you left there, when you were in Texas."

"Yeah, I know," Bud said in return, "but I have to remember why I left home in the first place."

"I think I see, you have to remember from the earliest before you get there," the agent replied.

They pulled into the driveway of Arlene's place. "Well Bud," said Bishop, "we seem to be on the same page. We'll just leave it at that. You've got my number, just give me a call when you come up with anything. Ok?"

"Yes sir, I'll do that," said Bud. He got out of the car and walked toward the house. When he got inside Arlene told him to call Jim

Tanner.

Jim answered the phone. "Hey, this is Bud, you called?"

"Yeah, can you make the run to Pine Bluff tomorrow?" Tanner asked.

"I can do that." Bud replied.

"Ok, meet me over at the store about seven-thirty," said Tanner. Bud hung up the phone.

"Well, I'm going to Pine Bluff again tomorrow," he told Arlene. She said "What do you bet the phone will ring in about five minutes?"

The phone rang again immediately. "Hey Bud, this is Jimbo, can I go to Pine Bluff with you?" the boy asked.

"Yeah, I guess so. Meet me at the store in the morning. You been working on those times tables?" Bud asked.

"Up to the nines. All right, I'll see you in the morning."

Bud went over to the store early, hoping to get a slice of persimmon pie to go with his coffee. Irene said, "Sorry, we used up all the persimmons."

Kenny came in right then and said, "There's more persimmons down there if you want to go down there and get 'em."

"No, thanks," said Bud, "I'd just as soon stay away from that place. Got any cinnamon rolls?"

Bud ate a cinnamon roll with his coffee and waited for Jim Tanner to arrive. Jimbo came in. "I got a question," said Jimbo. "If we've got calculators, why do we have to learn times tables?"

"Good question," said Bud. "It's ok to crunch the numbers with a calculator, but you're learning how math works when you learn how to do long multiplication and division. When you set up an equation, you have to know when to multiply or divide and add or subtract. But getting a ballpark idea, you really need your basic math skills to get there. And besides, what if your calculator is out of juice and you don't have a charger?"

"I don't know if I follow all that." said Jimbo.

"When we're on the road we can go over some things," said Bud. "You'll be surprised at how quickly you can put the pieces together."

After they loaded all the chickens into the truck, they headed out for highway seventy-one. Traffic wasn't heavy that time of day so they drove through Nashville and down to Hope. "Ok, Jimbo, what speed do we need to go to be traveling a mile a minute?"

"Sixty?" the boy replied.

"That's right," said Bud, "Do you see the mile markers on the side of the road?"

"Yeah, they're every mile."

"Well, from one marker to the next, you time it with your watch. If it takes sixty seconds you're going, what?"

"A mile a minute, or sixty miles an hour."

"Right. So if it takes only fifty-five seconds, how fast are you going?"

"Uh, sixty-five?"

"That's right. Every second less in time, a mile an hour faster."

"And every second longer, it's one mile slower. Wow," said Jimbo, "that's easy. But are speedometers pretty accurate?"

"No, they're not," Bud explained, "That's why you need to check it with the mile markers. Have you got a piece of paper?"

"Yeah, but I don't have anything to write with," Jimbo replied.

Bud said, "Here, take this pen. When I filled up with gas I checked the mileage. Write down eight, seven, five, eight, two, three."

"How much gas did you get?"

"Don't need that yet," said Bud. "When we get back this evening we'll subtract that mileage from the total, and we'll fill up with gas again."

Jimbo said, "I see, then we'll see how many gallons we use for that distance."

"You're, catching on," Bud said, "See, all this stuff is practical."

69

"Kenny's been telling me about algebra," said the boy, "it sounds like it'll be hard to do those story problems."

Bud replied, "Once you've got that figured out, the rest is easy. Now suppose you've got a word problem- and this is one you'll see- 'Mac filled his tank with gas and looked at his odometer. It read ten thousand and five. When he filled up the next time, it took ten gallons and his odometer read ten thousand two hundred and fifty. You could set that up couldn't you?"

Jimbo said, "It would be two hundred and forty-five divided by ten, wouldn't it?"

"Right on," said Bud, "In an equation it would be a fraction with two forty-five on top and ten on the bottom, and you just put a decimal point between the four and the five and you've got your mileage."

"Twenty-four point five," said Jimbo, "I'm not scared of algebra now."

"And I'll let you in on a little secret, you don't study math, you just do problems, and any math book has plenty of problems, with all the answers in the back. So when you're getting ready for a test, you do a few problems and if you can do 'em, you've got it down." Bud explained.

"What are we gonna do about lunch?" Jimbo wanted to know.

"When we get to the chicken plant, the ladies there have a fryer going with fresh chicken. They've got white bread and there's a pop machine there and we only need to buy the pop," said Bud, "so we can either eat while they're unloading or wait 'til we're on our way home."

"Why would we want to wait 'til later? Oh, I think I know, chicken plants don't smell too good, do they." Jimbo said.

"It's been my experience," Bud replied.

Chapter 10

Bobby slowed down when he saw a sign up ahead that read: 'Welcome to Arkansas.' "What next," he said idly. The next sign he saw said 'Dequeen eight miles.' As they got closer to the town Mrs. Graves looked at a street sign and said, "We're on Colin Raye Drive. It's like Ray Collins backwards."

Bobby said, "What a coincidence. Maybe it's a sign-- of something."

His grandmother said, "There was an actor named Ray Collins. He used to be on Perry Mason. He was Lieutenant Tragg."

"I'm at a loss," said Bobby, "We've come all this way, now we need to find somebody who likes licorice. It's a needle in a haystack."

"It puts it all in a new perspective, doesn't it?" Mrs. Graves commented.

"It sure does," said Bobby. "The one thing I know is that he always bought Twizzlers."

"There's a Walmart over on the right, that's as good a place as any to look," said his grandmother.

Bobby pulled over to the right, "But how many people are in that store?
Probably thousands."

"Maybe hundreds, but you said we've got to do something." said Viola.

Bobby drove into the parking lot and found a space fairly close to the store. They got out and started walking toward the entrance. "I'm searching my mind for what to say." said Bobby.

Mrs. Graves said, "Don't think about it- just start talking."

They walked by greeters who welcomed them to Walmart. "Where is the candy section?" Viola asked.

"Go toward the grocery department, I think it's in aisle three," said the woman. They walked to aisle three but it wasn't the candy section.

A female clerk said, "Can I help you find something?"

Bobby said, "I'm looking for Twizzlers licorice."

"Just follow me," said the woman. They soon arrived at an area with a wide variety of Twizzlers products.

"Actually," Bobby began, "I'm looking for a friend who always carries licorice with him."

The woman gave him a curious look, then she said, "Why don't you talk to the person who works in this section." She walked to the end of the aisle and said, "Joyce, come here a second."

Joyce soon arrived. "What can I help you with?"

Bobby drew a deep breath. "Actually I'm trying to track down a missing person who always carries Twizzlers licorice."

The woman chuckled, "You know, about a week ago somebody came in and bought twenty-four packages of licorice. I think it was for the Pine Valley Store."

"Where's that?" Bobby asked.

"West of here about five or six miles." she replied.

Mrs. Graves said, "Yeah, I remember passing the sign on the way in. Thank you so much"

"You're very welcome," Joyce replied.

On the way out of the parking lot Bobby said, "What does that tell you, about keeping the faith?"

"We just might be on the right track," his grandmother replied.

Bobby saw the sign that said 'Pine Valley' and they made their way down the narrow blacktop until they saw the store, parked, and walked inside. Dotty was sitting at the counter reading a magazine. "Help you folks?" she asked.

"We're looking for a man named Ray Collins." Bobby began.

Mrs. Graves added, "He's early middle-aged, dark hair, and, he likes licorice."

Dotty stared. "Oh my god." she paused, "Sit yourselves down, I have to call my boss. She picked up the phone and called. "Irene, can you come down here? There's some people here looking for somebody who likes licorice. A woman and a young man. Ok. She's coming down," she said as she hung up the phone. "Where are you folks from?" she asked.

"Wichita," said Bobby, "Ray went missing about a week ago."

Irene soon arrived. Bobby stood up, "Hi, I'm Bobby Dumford and this is my grandmother, Viola Graves. We're from Wichita."

Irene said, "I'm Irene Webb, and this is Dotty Cook. I may know the person you all are looking for, but people in Wichita weren't supposed to know where he is. Who told you he was here?"

Bobby said, "Nobody told us where he was. All they told us was that he was safe somewhere."

Mrs. Graves continued, "See, my grandson and Ray were pretty close. He searched through Ray's car and found a couple of scraps of paper that gave us a clue as to where to look."

Bobby continued, "We knew the car had been to Ardmore Oklahoma and we just searched west and east from there. And we had a big stroke of luck."

Irene was shaking her head in disbelief. "That covers the whole southern part of Oklahoma. Does anyone else know where you are?"

"Not a soul," said Bobby, "and trust me- we won't tell a soul." He was wiping back tears and so was Viola. Irene was shaking her head and dabbing at her eyes with a Kleenex.

"Ah, me," she said, "Ok, I think everything's fine. Bud- that's what we call him- is suffering from amnesia. He's been remembering a few things at a time. Maybe if he remembers you all, more will come back to him. This is just incredible. Just wait here for a while. Would you like some coffee?" Mrs. Graves nodded.

Dotty said, "They were looking for somebody that likes licorice."

"And a lady in the Walmart in Dequeen remembered that

somebody from Pine Valley bought a bunch of Twizzlers." said Bobby.

There was a moment of silence, then the door opened and Kenny came in carrying a bucket of persimmons. He walked toward the refrigerator and set the bucket on the floor. Irene said, "Kenny, put the persimmons in a bowl in the fridge and come over here and sit down." While he was doing that, she said, "This is my oldest boy, Kenny. He and Jimbo, my other boy, found our Bud down in the creek bottom and brought him up on horseback."

"Who are these folks, Mama?" he asked.

"This is Mrs. Graves and her grandson, Bobby. They just spent the last couple of days looking for Bud- they know him as Ray. They came here from Wichita, Kansas, where he went missing a week ago."

"Oh, Lord," said Kenny, "How did they know where he was?"

"They didn't," Irene explained. "But before we go through the whole story again, let's wait until Bud and Jimbo get back."

"He may not remember them," Kenny suggested.

"We'll just wait and see," said Irene. "Kenny, why don't you wait outside so Bud doesn't just drop Jimbo off and leave."

"Ok, but I don't know what to tell him," said Kenny.

"Just tell him I asked him to come inside," was Irene's reply, "Now please don't yell surprise," she added.

They soon heard the big truck driving in their direction. Anxious seconds passed. The door opened and Jimbo entered with Kenny and Bud close behind. Bobby was the first to speak, "Ray?"

Bud looked in his direction but didn't say anything for several seconds. Then he said, "Bobby, is that you?" Then he looked at Bobby's grandmother. "Viola? Did they tell you I was here?" She was wiping away tears as she got up and threw her arms around him.

"Nobody told us. Bobby found you…it's a long story," she

74

managed to say.

Irene was on the phone, "Arlene, it's Irene, can you come over here. I'll explain when you get here." Then she called Albert James and Dr. Barnes, deeming them to be the ones to fill out the necessary quorum to appropriately discuss their drop-in visitor's status. She sat down and heaved a sigh. Then she said, "There's two pizza crusts rising in the kitchen, would anyone volunteer to do the cooking?" Kenny and Jimbo both jumped to their feet. Kenny led the way to the kitchen.

Irene said, "I'm declaring the store closed, except for emergencies." Doc Barnes was the first to arrive, then Arlene, then Judge James. "I'll let Bobby fill you in on all the details," said Irene.

"I'm Bobby Dumford and this is my grandmother, Viola Graves. We're from Wichita, Kansas. Ray was a friend of ours, he lived a couple blocks away from us. He'd moved there about eight months ago. I went looking for him one afternoon, but he wasn't home and his car was gone. So, I called his boss and his boss said he didn't show up for work. That's not like him, so we got worried. A couple days went by and his car was back, but not Ray. Right away I checked out the car. There was light red mud on the tires and rims and I found a couple little scraps of paper on the floor. They were from a gas station in Ardmore, Oklahoma. Then, the next day, a tow truck came and got the car. We didn't know what was going on. About a week went by, then Mrs. Mabry, that's Ray's landlady, called and said the FBI had located Ray and he was safe where he was, but we couldn't contact him. Only Ray's boss and Mrs. Mabry, and we knew that the FBI had found him."

Albert James spoke up, "But you didn't know where he was?"

Bobby said, "No, all we knew was that that car had filled up with gas twice in Ardmore, Oklahoma. So, my grandmother and I drove down I-thirty-five, and went west on highway seventy and then east on seventy asking people if they'd seen anybody who bought any licorice."

Judge James chuckled, "He must have been somebody really special for you to go to that much trouble to find him."

"Well he is," said Mrs. Graves, "and it was truly a stroke of luck that we wound up here. Either that or a miracle."

"Miracles do happen," said the judge, "at least in our perception. But let me give a necessary precaution. For at least the time being, Ray can't go back to Wichita. There were people out to get him and there might still be. So for the immediate future, the story has to be that Ray- Bud to us- has no connection with Kansas. Does everybody understand?" They all nodded their agreement.

Irene spoke, "Let me say this so everybody understands. Bobby and Mrs. Graves are welcome here any time they want to come."

"Oh, we don't want to put any burden on you," said Bobby's grandmother.

"No, it's no burden, you're always welcome," said Irene.

Arlene spoke up, "I've got a spare bedroom at my house and all I do is keep watch on a herd of cattle which nearly anybody can do. Any friend of Bud's is a friend of mine."

Doc Barnes asked if he could put a word in, "Folks, here we are having a big group discussion and our neighbor, Bud, hasn't ever said what his plans are."

Bud looked up, "Thanks, Doc, but you know, I still feel like what Moses said, 'I'm a stranger in a strange land,' but, having said that, I'm just kind of overwhelmed. Ever since the Webb boys found me down in the creek bottom, there's just been folks that helped me every step of the way. Doc, and Judge James, Irene, the Tanners, Arlene, Perry, Fred, and on and on, everybody has tried to help me however they could." The room became very quiet. They were hanging on to every word Bud was saying. "As far as I can remember, I've just wanted to belong somewhere. If you folks will have me, I don't mind staying here where there's people who care about me."

The room was silent. Several were dabbing at their eyes. Kenny broke the silence, "Pizza's ready, who wants some?" The pizza was passed around. Few words were being said as they were all enjoying their pie. Then Judge James spoke.

"I think we can all agree that our Bud has found himself a niche in the community."

Arlene added, "Well since his recent arrival- albeit unintentional- he's been teaching us to make pizza, fixing broken pipes with old inner tubes, driving chickens to Pine Bluff, helping us animal caretakers, playing music for us on the keyboard, and just being an all-around good guy."

Doc chimed in, "I'll second the 'good guy' part. Why else would people have driven all over three states looking for him when he disappeared from their neighborhood?"

Albert James said, "Just to keep things in perspective, there is an FBI agent that's in contact with Bud in an on-going investigation to find out more about the criminal activity that caused his disappearance in the first place."

Bud was smiling and shaking his head. "It's just…it's just so much, I can't believe what a lucky man I am."

Kenny said, "About that FBI agent, if there's anything I could do to help with that, I'm willing to do that."

Jimbo chimed in, "Same here."

"Same here," said Bobby."

Judge James said, "Well we've got the Dumford and Webb Brothers junior detective agency. We've got to just stay low-profile until we hear from Agent Bishop. He's the professional, we're just amateurs."

Bud said, "But you said yourself that amateurs are just folks who are in it for the love."

Chapter 11

Ronnie Evers delivered uniforms for South Texas Laundry Service in Pasadena. He had a wife and one daughter. His favorite pastime was drinking beer and watching sports on TV. Over the years he had developed a routine that could that could potentially save lots of time and enjoyment for the average sports fan. He had plans to write an article for a big time magazine like Sports Illustrated. There were lots of commercial breaks in sports shows. By means of a little planning, a person could use the time consumed by the breaks for getting a cold beer out of the fridge or going to the bathroom to urinate. If the process used time wisely, a sports fan could avoid missing even a second of time in which active play, or commentary from the announcers was going on. He hadn't yet timed the commercials, but he had plans for that. His boss, Mr. Furumo, had told him that he had a special job for him on the weekend. On Thursday Mr. Furumo asked him to come to the office.

"Yeah, Ronnie, if you want to, you could pick up some overtime. I need somebody to drive up to Kansas City with a load of old starchy uniforms. Drive up on Saturday, stay overnight, and come back on Sunday. You interested?"

Ronnie said, "Yeah, I can do it."

"OK," said his boss, "I'll tell you how to get to the place you're driving to. They'll unload for you. Also, I need to have you take a quick trip to Columbia, Missouri. There's a place called 'Gino's Pizza', I just want to know if it's the same Gino who was in this area. Don't say nothin' to him. Don't say nothin' to anybody else. Just see if it's the same dude that was here. Can you handle that?"

"Yeah, I can do that."

"Ok, see me on Saturday morning and I'll get it all set up."

Gino Candiota had given himself a lot of time to decide where he would move himself, his wife, and his business. He had to stay in the pizzeria business, it was all he knew. He couldn't stay in South Texas. The Starrs wouldn't leave him alone. They insisted that he use their uniform business and buy his canned goods from them. The canned goods were low quality and he didn't need uniforms. All he wanted was to be left alone to run his business. After speaking to a lot of people, he came to understand that the trick was to do business in a place that didn't have a big mob related community. That left out big cities, and it left out coastal areas. He figured that three states away was a long enough distance. After discussing it with his wife, Millie, they decided on Columbia, Missouri. It was on I-seventy, about midway between St. Louis and Kansas City. He decided to keep the name simply, Gino's Pizza, but he added, And Neapolitan Kitchen. Colin Rayburn had given him the idea of renting a truck and moving all his kitchen equipment himself. He had put it all in a storage rental unit while he went about the process of finding a place to locate his restaurant.

He often thought about Colin, who kept encouraging him, and not letting him give in to the Starrs and all their henchmen. He felt remorse that Colin had put himself in danger to push back at Starr for what he had done to Gino. But Colin couldn't be dissuaded from testifying in court about what had happened. And Colin had gone into a witness-protection program all because of him. He didn't know where they had sent Colin, but he knew that someday he would hear from his friend.

After he got his neon sign installed, he went about taking care of all the details necessary to start selling pizzas. He had filled the back end of the rental truck with a lot of non-perishable items like canned tomato paste, big jars of olives, and sacks of high gluten flour. It was depressing to think about how the clientele he'd spent years building up, were just gone in a heartbeat and he'd have to start over from scratch in a new place, where nobody knew him. His new sign was visible from the interstate and read: Gino's Pizza and Neapolitan Kitchen. Four blocks south, take exit 26. It might pull in travelers, and it would be noticed by local people who were willing to try a local alternative to Pizza Hut and other chain restaurants.

Gino was working on the wiring to his dough mixer when Millie came in the store. He told her to sit down because there was something he needed to talk to her about. "I think I know what you want to talk about," she said. She didn't wait for his response, "You want to ask me if I'll help you in the kitchen until things get better." Gino nodded. "Of course I'll help in the kitchen. It's not your fault people tried to use you and cause you trouble." She stood up as Gino walked towards her.

"We'll be all right," he told her as he gave her a hug, "I just wish Colin was still with us, but he can't be. I just hope he's in a good environment, wherever he is. But he's a friendly sort of person, he'll find friends- he'll get along. I'm thinking, what we'll do, I can find wholesalers in KC or St. Louis to get my take-out boxes, my spices, my cheese. If I can just find a young guy with a car, he can make a run to a wholesaler, and evenings do deliveries."

Millie said, "You need to quit worrying. There's got to be young people around that need a job."

The first week he was open Gino made less than six pizzas a night, but by the next week he was making a dozen or more each night. He was open every day just to make as much money as he could. By the end of the next month there was a call from Colin. Millie answered the phone.

"Colin, it's good to hear from you, Gino's out buying paint right now."

"Good to know you guys are alive, how's Gino?" he asked.

"He's okay, he just worries too much. Listen, give me your phone number, I'll have him call you when he comes back in." She wrote the number on a pad by the phone, it was a three-one-six prefix, and put 'C.R.' next to it.

When Gino came back he carried two cans of paint in and put them behind the counter. He was still thinking about finding a young guy or two to do deliveries. "Call Colin," said Millie. "His number is next to the phone."

"Three-one-six, huh, wonder where that is." Colin answered on the first ring. "Hey dude, how did you know where I was?"

"Well, I knew it was Missouri and I knew it wouldn't be St. Louie or KC, so I looked at the map and Columbia was half way, so I called information and asked for Gino's Pizza." Colin explained.

"You should've been a detective. So, how are you anyway?" Gino asked.

"Oh, I'll blend in I guess. They got me a job, gave me a few bucks to get started. I bought an old Pontiac. There's an indoor mall here, I go over there and play a synthesizer in front of a music store. Already a couple of gals have given me their phone number. That's about it." Colin said.

"Life goes on I guess," Gino replied, "Where is this place anyway?"

"Wichita, Kansas. Not too far from you, you should come down some time."

"Or, you could come up here."

81

"No, can't do that, they want me to stay put for at least six months. They say it's safer that way." Colin explained.

"Well, anyway, you're ok and we're not far away," Gino put in, "Give us a call whenever, ok?"

"Yeah, I will, say hi to Millie. See ya Gino." Colin said, then hung up.

"So how is he?" Millie inquired.

"He's ok, he has to stay home for a while, so if we want to see him we'll have to go down there, to Wichita," said Gino. "Don't know when that'll be, sometime when we're not busy."

"Easter or Thanksgiving," said Millie with a laugh.

"Yeah, Easter or Thanksgiving," Gino agreed. He had picked up a few tips by observing how pizzeria chains ran their operations. They used dough rollers which were very much like old washing machine rollers. They used waste heat off of the kitchen to pump heat into the dining room. He had picked up a few tricks, but they couldn't compete with him when it came to the quality of the food.

One night there were several dine-in patrons at the tables. Gino saw that there were some young adults in the group. He made a point of asking them if they might be interested in delivering pizzas in their spare time. They said they weren't sure if they would have the time. "Well ok," he told them, "If you change your mind, just give me a call."

One man in the group said, "Can I use your phone?" Gino obliged him.

"Well, how is the pizza?" He asked the folks at the table.

"Never had any better," a middle aged man replied. The others nodded their heads in agreement. "Where did you learn the trade?" the man asked.

"In Naples," Gino replied, "the secret's in the crust and the baking. It was simpler there- not as many toppings. But I always use the best toppings I can get. Same with the olive oil and tomato paste- only the best. Please tell your friends. I plan to stay here a long time."

Millie chimed in, "Thank you all so much for coming to Gino's."

Chapter 12

It had been close to a month that Bud had been staying at Arlene's place. Since he'd been in Pine Valley he had been sleeping soundly for five or six hours a night. When he wasn't sleeping- just lying in bed, he had songs, or just music, going through his head. One night, lying on his back next to Arlene, he had a dream. He floated up-a few feet off the bed and drifted across the room. He looked back and could see himself still lying next to Arlene. He moved his arms like he was swimming but he could only move a few inches at a time. It was a little disturbing, because he knew his body was still asleep on the bed, but he didn't know what his consciousness was doing. He didn't want to wake up because he thought, perhaps, his memory was coming back. So he just kept floating. He started thinking of places where he'd slept in the past. There was his room at home in Indiana. Then he was stretched out on the seat of his deuce-and-a-half. Then there was a mobile home and he was with a woman. Who was she? Her name was Lena, but he didn't feel like talking to her. He remembered that she had to choose between him and her dad and her dad won. He remembered her dad's name was Al Eberle. The old guy was into gulf coast engineering- whatever that was. Then there was a small room in the back of a restaurant, and there was an apartment with the kitchen in the same room as the bedroom and he had to climb a flight of stairs.

He felt somebody grab his arm. "Bud, what's going on? You're waving your arms around."

He came awake. "Ahh…sorry Arlene, I must have been dreaming, what time is it?"

"Four in the morning, are you ok?" she asked.

"Yeah, yeah. You just go back to sleep, I'll tell you about it in the morning." Bud got up and walked into the kitchen. He sat down

84

at the table and looked around for a piece of paper and a pen. There was a pen in a coffee mug on the table and he pulled a paper towel off the roll on the wall. Then he took a deep breath and closed his eyes for a few seconds. Then he opened his eyes and he wrote down: Lena, Al Eberle, truck, mobile home, Starr, Gino, and Cleveland. Then he thought for a minute. Sequence- it was out of sequence. He realized he was still sleepy.

Should he make coffee? No, it's too early for coffee. He'd written down what came to him. Then he thought about seeing himself lying next to Arlene. He didn't want to leave her. "She's better than that whole bunch of Texas people put together," he told himself, "except for Gino and Gino's wife." He looked at the clock. It was five AM and he realized he was still sleepy. He walked carefully back into the bedroom, so as not to disturb Arlene, and laid down on the bed. In two minutes he was fast asleep.

Pete Bishop had an idea. It was based on his training for his job. There was information that could be obtained by just being a fly on the wall in certain places in the Houston area. It was a crying shame that the guys that had picked Colin to testify against Starr hadn't found out more about Colin in the first place. But, all the same, Colin- or Bud as he came to be known- would have been acquainted with quite a few people in his old haunts. There were three teen-aged boys that might be of some help in that regard. He just had to discuss the idea with a few interested people. He called Mr. Rogers, the Arkansas AG.

"I've got an idea about getting a little background on the man in Pine Valley. The one we call Bud."

"What's your idea?"

"If we could get somebody who could get close to people in the Houston area- who knew him when he was living there- just on a casual basis."

"Oh, I think I see what you're driving at. What comes to mind is pool halls and barber shops."

"We've got three teenagers who are eager to help, but school will be starting soon," said Bishop, "Maybe they can help out by filling in for some ambitious soul who could do the field work. Well, I just now started thinking about it, so I'll get back with you if I think of some approach we could take." said Pete.

"All right, let me know what you come up with."

Pete Bishop called Albert James and Dr. Barnes to fill them in on his idea for searching out Bud's background.

The jam that Saturday was at Fred's place. Dr. and Mrs. Barnes had expressed a desire to be there, and all the music-playing regulars were there. They had been playing for about an hour and were in the midst of playing fiddle tunes when an idea came to Doc. There must be people all over the country doing this very thing, so somewhere in the Houston area there must be people jamming like the people here. He decided to have a chat with Fred whenever he had a chance.

Later that evening, Doc found Fred in his kitchen. He told him of his idea. "If I could get you and Bud and Albert James to come sit down and talk together, I think we can come up with a plan to get the information we need without any danger or difficulty," he told Fred, "I'm pretty sure, in a populated area like that, there will be what they call 'open mikes', in a cocktail joint where they have paid musicians on weekends, but one day during the week they let amateurs get up and play. When you're there, you ask around to find out where there's a regular weekly jam. Do you follow?"

"Ah, yes." said Fred.

"Then at the jam you can just casually ask around about our Bud. But we need to have Bud in on this before we do anything. Would you be free tomorrow afternoon?"

Fred smiled, "Yeah, call me around four. This sounds interesting."

When Doc got home he called Albert James to fill him in on his idea for picking up information about Bud. The judge said, "We need to talk to that fellow Bishop about this first."

"This was an idea of his to begin with," said Doc, "I just came up with the idea of a musicians jam. We'll check with him and make sure everything's ok before we start this whole project,"

"I'll call him and let him know about the plan," the judge replied.

"Ok, Albert, get back with me after you talk to him," said Doc, "Oh, by the way, who is Bud now anyway?"

"Carl Russell," said Albert.

"Oh, yeah," said Doc, "thanks, I'll talk to you later."

On Sunday afternoon, Fred, Sarah and Kate showed up at Dr. Barnes' place. Ida Barnes had brewed up a large pitcher of sweet iced tea. Albert James was also there, along with Bud and Arlene. They were all sipping tea when Doc asked, "What about Pete Bishop?"

"I spoke with him earlier," said the judge, "We can work out what we need to do, but we'll give him a report before we do anything."

"All right," said Doc, "Anybody want to start?"

Bud said, "To start with, this is a weekday thing we're talking about."

"The open mike or the jam?" asked Fred.

"Both," said Bud, "People make all kinds of other plans on weekends, so they do this on a weeknight and on a more-or-less regular basis."

"I see," said Fred, "any idea where some of these places might be?"

"I think," Arlene began, "We might be able to find somebody who's been there who is a guitar picker. Maybe in a music store in Texarkana we might find a clue about that."

"That's worth a shot," said Kate, "I've got a doctor's appointment tomorrow, I'll just stop by Guitar Headquarters and see what they can tell me."

Doc said, "Bud, anything you'd like to suggest, we're glad to hear it."

"I think it would be helpful if you didn't ask any questions until you get to an actual jam. Then, as the evening wears on, just ask if anybody knows of a keyboard player named Colin. Just say you met him in New Orleans, or San Antonio, and he said he was from around Houston. Hopefully some of them have heard of me. If they haven't, I guess you have to find another jam."

"But would there be another jam?" Fred asked.

"Oh, sure," said Bud, "there might even be another jam the next night and one of the people at the jam you're at will be going to the other jam."

"So, it sounds like," said Judge James, "a good conversationalist would be the best person to do this. I think the best approach would be not to sound like a private eye. So who's the best conversationalist in the group?"

Kate said, "Sarah," as she nodded in Sarah's direction. Fred and Kate both nodded in agreement.

"Well, Sarah," said Kate, "what do you think?"

"I think, all of a sudden I got myself into something, but, I left myself open for it," Sarah replied. "Let's take it one step at a time. Kate goes to the music store in Texarkana to, kind of, make a connection with Houston. I'm going to need a lot of support if I'm going to do this. Who's going with me?"

Fred said, "I'll go. My customers can get along without me for a few days, and I need a change of scene for a while."

88

Fred had a service station and garage. Part of having him do mechanical work was buying ten gallons of gas from him. Lots of people bought gas from him for their lawn mowers and chain saws, but he needed to sell a volume of gas to be able to do that.

"I'll keep the station open while you're gone," said Bud. I can do a few things on vehicles, and I'm sure Kenny and Jimbo can help me out."

Dr. Barnes said, "We haven't mentioned any financial plans yet. I just want to say, of course there'll be money spent. But we've got enough people involved that it's not going to be a big thing. We'll split the costs among all of us, ok?"

"Oh, sure," said Kate, "We'll all pitch in. It won't be a hardship on anybody."

Bud was shaking his head as he often did. "I feel like I ought to say something. But..."

Arlene said, "I think I know, but you can't put it in words." Bud smiled and nodded his head.

"Should we try to call Pete Bishop," he asked.

"Wouldn't hurt," said the judge, "Let's let Bud talk to him first."

Lindy Barnes handed Bud the phone. It rang twice before Pete answered. "Bishop."

"Hi Pete, this is Bud in Pine Valley. We've got a plan, would you like to hear it," said Bud.

"I'm all ears," Pete replied.

"Ok, it was Doc's idea, but several of us talked it over and we pretty much agree on how we can do it. We have this musicians' group, and we're pretty sure we can find a similar group in the Houston area. We'll start by finding an open mike at a beer joint. Once we're there..."

"Hold it, Bud, who're we talking about?" Pete wanted to know.

"Oh, not me," Bud replied. "Just two of our group, probably Sarah and Fred. If they just visit a sizable music store they can easily find an open mike."

"Mike who?" asked Pete.

Bud chuckled, "No, not a person. Open microphone. See they have paid entertainment on the weekend, but one night a week they let people get up and play. So, they won't ask any questions there, except where is there a weekly jam like the one we have here in Pine Valley. So when they locate a jam, then they can go there, and, at some point just casually ask, 'Have you ever heard of Colin who plays keyboard, I met him once in New Orleans, or San Antonio, or wherever.'"

Pete didn't say anything for several seconds. "Man, that's really good thinking. I would have never thought about anything like that. If it works, and I don't see why it wouldn't, it could be a whole new way to get information. Just a few little things to see if we're on the same page. Any strangers they talk to, don't tell them any real names. And try to keep notes of addresses they go to. Any questions?"

"Not at the present, but I've got your number and I'll fill you in on any details later on," said Bud.

"Good man, and, by the way, this could mean a whole lot about your future security," said Pete, "Bye for now."

"Goodbye, and thanks," Bud replied.

Judge James said, "What are we going to do with respect to transportation?"

"Well, we're going to drive down there," said Fred.

"Yes, but what do we do about the tag?" the judge asked. "Might I suggest you rent a car somewhere like Marshall, Texas. That way no one is going to notice an Arkansas tag and wonder how it got there."

Doc said, "I'll let you borrow a visa card for that and gas too. Just bring the receipts back and we'll split the expenses."

Judge James said, "I've taken down a page of notes. Can we get back together in a couple of days and see if the process is going along?"

Sarah said, "That's fine by me, anyone else?" The rest nodded their approval as they rose to head for home.

As Arlene and Bud were on their way home, Arlene said, "I sure hope this scheme works out."

"Well, I do too," Bud replied, "but whatever happens, these people did their level best to do what they could."

"That's true," Arlene agreed, "How do you feel about sausage and cole slaw for supper?"

"Could you throw in some grits?" said Bud, "I've taken a liking to that stuff."

"I can do grits. You know, Doc Barnes told me once that grits helped solve a public health problem," said Arlene.

"What kind of health problem?" Bud asked.

"There were a bunch of people in the south that suffered from pellagra. They didn't know if it was an infectious disease or what. So somebody was looking into their diet, and they found out that the only bread they ate was corn bread. Then they noticed that some people used their corn to make hominy and grits, and those people didn't have pellagra. So they finally figured out that pellagra was caused by a vitamin deficiency. There's vitamins in corn, but just grinding it doesn't release them from the grain. But if they soaked the corn in wood ashes and rainwater, like making soap, and turned the corn into hominy, they never got pellagra," Arlene explained."

"But, don't some Mexican people just have corn?" Bud replied.

"Yes, but they use limestone to grind the corn, and that brings out the vitamins," said Arlene.

Sarah had been teaching guitar to many children and a few adults in the community. She had taught Maggie for over a year and Kate for several months. Both Kate and Maggie would tell people that most of what they knew about guitar they learned from Sarah, and along the way, taught them how to get the most out of their singing voices. Fred was married to Maggie and had also learned a lot about music from Sarah, but, pretty much on an informal level. Maggie didn't mind Fred going to Texas with Sarah, they were old friends. She told Kate, "If you can't trust an old friend, then who can you trust?"

The plan was for Maggie to drive Fred and Sarah to a car rental place in Texarkana. They wanted to make sure the car had a Texas tag. They loaded all their stuff into the back of Fred's station wagon. Fred brought his Washburn mandolin, and Sarah brought her Taylor guitar. They decided to be a garage owner and a guitar teacher from Baton Rouge who were just taking a few days off to visit the Gulf Coast of Texas. Kate had tried a music store but she didn't learn much. They stopped at a music store just off State Line Ave. Fred walked up to a young lady at the counter and asked for a set of D'adario mandolin strings. While he was paying for his strings he said, "We're going down to the Houston area and we were wondering if they have any places with an open mike."

"I'm not sure," she replied, "but let me make a phone call to this guy that used to live down there." She picked up the phone and punched in a number. "Yeah, Tommy, it's Carla at Texas Strings. Is there a joint around Houston that has an open mike?" She wrote something down. "Yeah, OK thanks." Then she said, "There's a place called the Purple Door on Westheimer Road. They have an open mike on Monday night."

Fred said, "OK, great. Thanks a lot."

When they were back in the car Fred said, "I'm getting kinda nervous thinking about acting,"

"Well, just be a nervous person," said Maggie, "you do that quite well."

Sarah said, "I did some theater myself, if you do a really good acting job, somebody will think you're an actor and not a garage owner. So, just act like a garage owner."

"That sounds easy. Why didn't I think of that?" said Fred.

"Try not to think, you'll do fine," said Sarah, "I'll do most of the talking."

"You always do," said Maggie.

"Not always, most of the time, but not always," Sarah replied.

"But are you nervous about it?" Fred wanted to know.

"Actually I'm not," said Sarah.

"Great, that's one thing we've got under control," said Fred.

It was mid-morning when they reached a rental car place on the Texas side- to be sure they would have a Texas tag.

They rented a ninety-three Chevy Nova. It was blue and was fairly non-descript in appearance. Fred and Sarah said goodbye to Maggie who told them, "Whatever you do, be careful."

"That's easy," said Sarah, "I've got no problem with careful."

Sarah took the first turn driving. "What do you think about staying off the interstates?" she asked Fred.

"I don't think they would help us either distance or time anyway," he replied, "We can stay on US fifty-nine the whole way."

"That's fine," Sarah agreed, "won't even have to look at the map. Say, what kind of music do you think we'll be playing?"

"That's a good question. We can rule out classical- also hip-hop; besides that, it could be anything," said Fred. "You do a lot of jazz. I do a lot of bluegrass and folk. It might be interesting to find out what we do play. Then we can tell the folks back home what we did."

"What kind of food are you inclined to want to try?" Sarah asked.

"At my age in life I've gotten to the point that I take advantage of the chains. If I see a Waffle House, I know what they've got and I know what to order. But, I'm not afraid to go somewhere local if…"

"If there's a lot of cars in the parking lot?"

"Yeah, that's it," Fred replied. They both laughed.

"What's always amazed me," said Fred, "is how much better maintained the roads are in Texas than in Arkansas."

"Let me ask you something," Sarah began, "Out of all things you know about, what made you decide to run a garage?"

"Have you read 'Zen and the Art of Motorcycle Maintenance'?"

"No, but I've heard of it."

"Well this fellow Pirsig, wanted to get into philosophy, but the teachers wouldn't let him discuss the philosophy, only the philosophers. He got so stressed out about it, it was driving him crazy. But by doing something as down-to-earth as working on his motorcycle kept him in touch with reality. Does that make any sense?" Fred explained.

"You mean dealing with the concrete keeps you from getting lost in the abstract?" said Sarah.

"Exactly, everything has to do what it's supposed to. Not like people who are so unpredictable."

Maggie and Kate were discussing the upcoming Saturday jam. Maggie said, "You know, I keep thinking about a song."

"What song is that?" Kate inquired.

"Oh, it's not a song yet. As far as I know there hasn't ever been a song about Pine Valley, and what's been going through my mind is, 'When I first came to Pine Valley, I was a man without a name. Didn't know where I was going, or the place from where I came'."

Kate didn't say anything for several seconds, then she said, "Can I participate?"

"Oh sure," Maggie replied. "I know, let's just leave it at that and wait until anybody wants to add to it."

"Good idea. What does it make you think of?" Kate asked.

"When first unto this country, a stranger I came." said Maggie.

Jimbo was at the cash register ringing up a sale when Kenny came in.

Kenny said, "Are you putting thirty weight oil in Oscar's car?"

"Yeah, that's what he wanted."

"You don't mind if I talk to him do you?"

"Be my guest, he's over in the store."

Oscar was having a cup of coffee when Kenny walked in. "Mr. Brand, did you have a reason to put straight thirty weight oil in your car?"

"Ah, I've heard it holds up better than a multi-grade," Oscar replied.

"No, actually, what breaks down first is the light oil. For instance, you take 10W40 oil, when it's cold, it acts like a 10 weight and the hotter it gets it becomes 40 weight. Then as it ages, the low viscosity factor goes away and it becomes a 40 weight oil." Kenny explained.

Oscar said, "You mean 10W40 would protect an engine better than straight 30 weight?"

"Yep, and it's the same price."

"Well I'll be darned. Ok, just put 10W40 in it."

When Kenny got back to the station he called out, "Hey Jimbo, put 10W40 in Oscar's car."

"You got it. Notice how this oil has a greenish tint to it?" Jimbo mused.

"Must be something about the ingredients that make it thin when it's cold," Kenny replied. "Check his differential and see if it has enough fluid in it."

Jimbo said, "I hope ol' Fred's having fun in Texas."

"He's bound to be," said Kenny, "He doesn't have to work and gets to play his mandolin all he wants."

Bud dropped by the station later that afternoon. "How are things going?" he asked.

"Pretty good," Kenny replied, hey, I've got a question for you."

"Shoot," said Bud.

"Why do they say 'tuning up' an engine? You're changing the plugs and so forth, but why is it called tuning up?" Kenny asked.

"It's actually just setting the timing that's called tuning. I guess it comes from tuning strings on an instrument. If the tension isn't right it sounds bad. If your engine's out of tune it also sounds bad." Bud related.

"Well, OK, what's the timing?" Kenny asked.

"OK, it really refers to the exact moment when the spark ignites the fuel. Let me draw you a picture." Bud found a piece of paper and a pen. He drew a picture of a piston and connecting rod inside a cylinder with a spark plug at the top. "The four strokes are: intake, compression, power and exhaust. Now this piston is coming up on compression stroke. You want the plug to fire when the piston is in the exact right place to get maximum power on power stroke. You do that by setting the distributer and tightening it in place. The old way they did it was by sound and feeling the vacuum on the carburetor. Now we do it with a strobe light that blinks when the spark is going to number one cylinder. In a few years all the engines will have electronic timing which won't need to be adjusted. Make sense?"

"So it helps for the distributer to be new and the plugs to be clean."

"Right, and also for the wires to be in good condition, and also the ignition coil." Bud explained, "in addition to the valves being adjusted and the carburetor in good condition."

"Wow," said Jimbo, "that's a lot of stuff to know how to do."

96

"Of course the best way to learn it is to do it. If you get a tune up while Fred's away give me a call. If you don't, then get Fred to show you the next time he does one. And I'll tell you something to always keep in mind whenever you're working with tools." Bud said.

"What's that," Kenny asked.

"Every move you make with a tool, make sure you're not going to cut or bruise yourself. You got issued ten fingers when you were born and you can't get any replacements." Bud replied. "I'm always aware of that because I play keyboards, but everybody should have ten fingers."

"But carburetors are always causing problems," said Kenny.

"Basically they just mix gas with air, that's what the jets do. Personally I just get a rebuilt one when they start messing up. Some day they all will have injectors," said Bud.

Kenny said, "I've got a story you might like."

"I'm all ears," Bud responded.

"Well, there was this black mechanic that lived in Antoine. He specialized in Pontiacs. His name was Billy. There was this lady, lived in Delight, named Phyllis Craig. She had a Pontiac. When it came inspection time she took it to Billy 'cause she knew he would be lenient. So she drives to Antoine and she pulls into Billy's place and she's talking to Billy. Then another Pontiac pulls in and the driver gets out and is leaning against his car. Then Billy says, 'Phyllis, this might not be a good time to do this.' She says, 'Why?' He says, 'That might be the man from Little Rock that checks out the inspectors.' Phyllis glances over, 'Nah, Billy that's not the man from Little Rock, that's Glen.' Billy says, 'Who?' She says, 'Glen Campbell.' See, he saw a white guy in a suit, he thought it had to be the state inspector."

"That's funny," says Bud, "That's what we always get, thinking that the other race all look alike."

Chapter 13

Sarah and Fred were approaching Houston. They stopped at a Walmart where they could either get directions or get a good map of the area. They found a really nice Rand McNally map of the area. They got on the freeway, found the right exit and located Westheimer Rd. The Purple Door was a short distance away. After locating the club they found a Best Western Motel. They asked for a non-smoking room and it was on the second floor.

As they were taking their bags up to the room, Fred remarked, "I'd like to think of this as being a vacation."

"Well, you should," Sarah replied, "You're away from home, staying in a rented room, you've got your mandolin and we're going to play music, what else could you ask for?"

"You're right, I've got all that, but I can't get over being a detective."

"You need to forget that," said Sarah, "you don't have to cross examine anybody. Just every little once in a while say 'Ever heard of a keyboard player named Colin?' -just the first name- and then it's all listening. So just keep thinking 'listen'."

Fred said, "You know, I think I can do that. Now what about getting something to eat, or should we wait 'til we get to the Purple Onion?"

"That's Purple Door. Nah, we don't know what their food is like, let's check out the café across the street, you know what I always say?"

"Yeah, if it has a lot of cars parked outside, it has to be good."

That night at the Purple Door Fred and Sarah came in just after six o'clock. They were carrying a guitar and a mandolin. The bartender said, "You look like musicians, did you come to play?"

Sarah said, "That would be a great song title. I'm Sarah and this is Fred."

"I'm Levi. Write your names down on this clipboard. We'll be kicking things off around seven. Would you like a drink? You get one free if you walk in here with an instrument."

"What do you have on tap?" Fred asked.

"Michelob and Pabst," Levi said.

"We'll take one of each," Fred replied.

The stage was in a corner by the front window. There were a couple of mikes and a small pa system.

It wasn't long before a tall man carrying a guitar case entered the building. His name was Jay and he ordered a bottle of Budweiser. Fred thought it was odd that a man would order a bottle of Bud when there was Michelob on tap, but he knew well there was no accounting for taste. When Jay saw Sarah and Fred he walked over and introduced himself.

"You folks from around here?" he asked.

Sarah said, "No, we're from Baton Rouge."

"Know any Cajun songs?" he asked.

Fred said, "Well I can follow along with a lot of those songs, but I don't know any lyrics. I know Jambalaya, if you consider it a Cajun song."

"Oh, hell," Jay replied, "that's Hank Williams, but I've heard that the Cajuns adopted it as one of their own. I'll do it tonight if y'all want to join in."

"Suits me fine," said Sarah.

A couple of young women came in carrying a bass guitar and a fiddle. Jay allowed that they were the Robison sisters who sang beautiful harmonies and that they played in their church regularly and came to the Purple Door occasionally. "It's our lucky day," he added.

By this time, about a dozen people had filtered into the club.

Sarah started by singing Wayfaring Stranger. She was hoping to attract the attention of the Robison sisters and it seemed to work. Fred played a lead on the mandolin and the small crowd showed their appreciation.

Jay played mostly Hank Williams songs. He asked Sarah to come up and help him with Jambalaya. It turned out to be a crowd pleaser.

The Robison sisters were Anne and Elise. Anne played Farther Along on the fiddle while Elise accompanied her on a Fender P-bass. Then they sang the song acapella into one microphone. Sarah was a little surprised when they asked if she knew Hard Times by Stephen Foster. She joined them and they did a killer rendition in three-part harmony. The crowd were on their feet cheering by the time they finished the song. Fred and Sarah each had another beer provided by the music fans.

Later they asked Jay if he knew of a jam at a person's home. "There's a guy named Chubby- it's at his house. The name of the jam group is the Skillet Likkers, named for an old country band that recorded together back in the twenties. I'll draw you a little map of how to get to Chubby's place, and I'll call and tell 'em y'all are coming."

When they were back in the hotel room Sarah told Fred she would love to work with the Robison sisters if circumstances were different. "Yeah, I know just what you're feeling," Fred replied, "who knows what'll happen in the future, but you've got that 'if only' thing going on in your mind."

Arlene came in while Bud was drinking coffee. "You got a letter from Bobby." She handed it to him. "Must be several pages she said."

Bud opened it and started reading. He didn't say anything for several minutes.

Arlene said, "It's not bad news is it?"

"No. Here, I'll read it to you. 'Dear Bud, hope everything is going well. I've got this idea I've been thinking about. You're pretty good at math, maybe you could help me get a handle on this thing. I think most of us are competing with each other and cooperating with each other at the same time. It's not about anybody in particular, just the whole human race."

Bud closed his eyes and shook his head. Arlene was frowning.

"Keep reading," she said, "he's got my attention now."

Bud continued, "Now you take the NFL. It's a big organization and it's a huge cooperative endeavor. They've got all these commissioners, and these teams, and these owners and all these players. They're all cooperating to make this process happen. And it's all for competition, and it's for entertainment, and they all have to follow strict rules. And in that draft, they're bending over backwards to give every team an equal chance to get the best players they can so the games can be as competitive as possible. But then all these owners are trying as hard as they can to get the players that can stomp all over their opponents. Then the players are competing with their teammates to be on the first string, but in the game they're cooperating with those guys to beat their opponents. And the first string guys are telling the second string guys how to play better so when they're in the game they'll play better."

Arlene held up her hand, "Whoa, hold it, I can't think as fast as you're reading. How long is this thing?"

"Another page, and, I must confess, I don't see where he's going with this."

"Well, read on." Arlene replied.

"And then, there are all the rules. You can't run into the kicker. You can't grab the face mask, you can't go out of bounds, and the officials have to enforce all that. It's just fascinating, that at the same time, somebody is cooperating in several different ways, and competing in several different ways. Now, what I'm trying to figure out is, when you take this whole thing all together, what's happening more, is it cooperation or competition? Not just how often, but to what level?

Can you break it down to each individual and to a group? Can there be a percentage of one or the other? It isn't hard to describe it, but can you quantify it? The NFL is just one example. It isn't just about sports. The same thing is going on all around us. There's business, government, everything we do has this stuff going on. I'd be interested in knowing what your reaction is to all this. Your friend, Bobby."

"Whew," said Bud, "I don't have a clue."

"That kid does a lot of thinking. Not that that's a bad thing, and he's exercising his brain," Arlene commented, "I wonder what he thinks you can do to help him."

"Well he's impressed with my use of math. Trouble is, you can't just set up an equation like you do with time, donuts, speed, and weight. There's no way to quantify anything. And I have a feeling that a lot of people in the field of behavior are looking at what he's talking about. Next chance I get I'll ask Doc Barnes if he knows anything about it."

"There's so much that's of a subjective nature," Arlene added, "just think how much instant replay affects the nature of it." Bud broke into a laugh.

"Yes, and think how much cheerleaders affect the outcome." They both started laughing and couldn't stop for several minutes.

Sarah and Fred arrived at Chubby's place around seven. Chubby said, "C'mon in guys, Jay told me you were coming. Most of these folks won't get here 'til eight or eight-thirty but that's okay. There's snacks on the kitchen table and there's drinks in the cooler, so help yourselves."

"How long have you all been playing together?" Fred asked Chubby.

"Since the early seventies," Chubby replied, "around twenty-four years, I guess."

"I'm wondering what kind of music to expect," said Sarah.

"Well, y'all were at the Purple Door last night, we do a lot of the stuff they do down there. But, really, it's almost anything. Some play mostly country. Others play folk, rock, blues, church music… you never know what some of them will come up with." Chubby related.

"Sounds like my kind of people," Sarah commented.

A tall, slender woman entered the room. "Hi, I'm Chubby's wife, Alicia."

"Pleased to meet you" said Sarah.

"I'm not a musician myself," said Alicia, "I just like to listen."

"That's great," said Fred, "it's always better when there's people that just listen."

"And I've noticed," Sarah said, "that the couples where the spouse is also at the jam, have a much closer relationship than the ones who aren't"

"Yeah, we've noticed that too," said Chubby.

Over the next hour the room filled with Texas musicians. Most were carrying guitar cases, but there were a few fiddles, as well as a lap dulcimer, a banjo and an autoharp. Jay was there doing his Hank Williams renditions. They later learned that he was also an auctioneer. The youngest musician on the scene was named Barry Duncan. He played Red-Haired Boy on a three-quarter size fiddle. There were at least four guitars accompanying him.

Sarah told Fred she would be out in the kitchen trying to strike up a conversation. She met a woman named Carla and another named Belinda. She learned that they were non-musicians who were there with their husbands. She decided it was time to throw

103

out the chum. "Do either of you know of a keyboard player by the name of Colin?"

"Is he sort of tall and dark?" asked Carla. Sarah nodded. "Where do you know him from?"

Sarah said, "I ran into him in New Orleans, once. He said he was from the Houston area."

Belinda said, "I think he moved away somewhere. As a matter of fact, the kid playing the fiddle, Barry? Well, Colin was friends with his folks, the Duncan family. They could tell you more about him than anyone else could."

"Thanks," said Sarah, "I'll do that. I just love kids that are so into music. You just think, oh boy, what will they sound like later on."

"I know what you mean," said Carla. "My husband says that kids that take music lessons are usually better in school than other kids."

"Oh, it's true," said Sarah, "I teach guitar myself. A kid that starts taking lessons and stays with it, usually does well in all their other subjects. Excuse me, folks, I'm going to get back to the music."

As Sarah entered the living room Fred said, "It's your time girl, give us a tune." Sarah struck a minor chord and started singing.

"I'm just a poor wayfarin' stranger, travelin' through this world of woe…And there's no sickness, toil nor danger, in that bright world to which I go…" Fred played along on his mandolin and when they came to "I'm goin' there to meet my mother…" three other people joined her in harmony. When the song was finished there was loud applause.

Carla spoke up, "When it's my turn I want to hear Sarah sing 'Hard Times' by Stephen Foster."

Chubby said, "It's your turn now. Sarah, can you sing that?"

104

Sarah said, "I do it acapella, anyone who wants to harmonize is welcome. 'Let us pause in life's pleasures and count our many fears, for we all share sorrow with the poor. There's a song that will linger forever in our ears, oh hard times come again no more." When she got to, "It's the song, the sigh of the weary…" the rest of the room joined in. Sarah got another big round of applause. She looked at Barry Duncan, then glanced around the room. There was another fiddle player who bore a strong resemblance to Barry and she knew it must be his father. When the man headed toward the kitchen she followed him.

"Are you Mr. Duncan?" she asked.

"Yeah, I'm Bob Duncan. Say, you've got a beautiful voice, do you live around here?"

"No, we're from Baton Rouge, just in town for a couple of days. They told me you were acquainted with a guy named Colin that plays keyboard."

"Oh yeah, I remember him. My boy knows him better than I do."

"Well, could I get your phone number so I could talk to Barry, or you, or your wife, about him?"

"Oh, sure, here's my card, I know Barry was sort of mystified that he just sort of disappeared."

"Well, I'll call and we can exchange notes and maybe come up with something."

"All right, yeah, I'm sure my son would like to talk with you. Thanks."

Sarah and Fred left around ten thirty. There were still ten or so people there but they were anxious to talk about what they'd learned.

Sarah said, "You know, I'd bet a person could go nearly anywhere in this country and do what we just did."

"Yeah, you mean finding people to jam with?" Sarah nodded. "But what did you find out?" Fred wanted to know.

105

"Several of them were acquainted with Bud, and they knew he'd left the area, but that's about it. Now the Bob Duncan family, and their boy, Barry, were a little better acquainted with him. Bob gave me his card so we can talk to him later. I think if we chat with them, between what we know, and what they know, we might be able to find out more."

"That sounds reasonable to me," said Fred, "let's wait and see what we can find out."

The next morning, after coffee and bagels in the lobby they decided to visit a music store. After a bit of driving around they saw a place called 'Great Southern Music.' The place had lots of acoustic and electric guitars, plus everything you needed to supply a working band. They were looking at mandolins when Sarah said, "Talking to those ladies last night we got into the subject of couples that come to the jams together."

"Yeah, what did they say?" Fred asked.

"Oh, the usual observation about how they've got a stronger relationship. But I remembered something that happened a while back. There was this guy that played mandolin, and he and his wife were at the Gibson factory in Nashville where he was having them look over his A-model. So, while the luthiers were checking out his instrument, they were in the display room looking at all the F-models."

"I bet it was a bit overwhelming."

"It was, and then his wife said, 'Why don't you take one down and play it?' So he says, 'well, you know, I don't need more than one mandolin.'
And she says, 'yes you do.' Just three words, 'yes you do.' Now, is that a good relationship?"

Fred was nodding his head, "Yeah, that's a good relationship right there. I just wish more people would realize that. You know, I just thought about something when we came in here."

"What's that," Sarah asked.

"We could have started in a place like this. Talked to some people." Fred replied.

"Yeah, but we would ultimately be getting down to a club or a jam," said Sarah. She turned to the clerk at the counter. "Could I use your phone?"

"Local call? Sure."

She called Bob Duncan's number. "This is Bob, how can I help you?"

"This is Sarah Parker, the guitar player."

"Oh, sure. Would you all like to come over and talk, maybe this evening?"

"That would be great. We're at Great Southern music right now. Is there anything you folks need in the way of music, while we're here?"

"Oh, I think Barry could use a piece of rosin if they've got it."

"We can do that. About what time tonight?"

"Oh, after five. My home address is on the card."

"All right, we'll see you later on."

Sarah bought a piece of Bella Fina, the best rosin they had. She thought maybe it would stick in Barry's mind if he had some good rosin to play his fiddle with.

Fred and Sarah arrived at the Duncan home at five after five. Linda Duncan met them at the door. "Hi, I'm Linda," she said, "Come on in and make yourselves at home. I hope you like pizza, Bob is bringing some home." She called upstairs, "Barry, Sarah and Fred are here."

"Ok, Mom, I'll be right down," he called back.

They sat in the living room and talked about Barry's fiddle playing. Bob arrived a few minutes later and they went into the small kitchen and sat down at the table. As they were passing around the pizza, Bob Duncan started the conversation.

"Apparently, we all know Colin. You folks want to know what

happened to him while he was here, and we want to know what happened to him after he left here. Am I right?"

Sarah started, "That pretty much describes us. Now let me say this, Colin has never done anything to anybody that he needs to apologize for." Bob, Linda, and Barry all smiled and nodded.

Barry said, "Can I just ask you if he's all right?"

"Oh sure," said Sarah, "he's safe and sound where he is, the reason we're here is to try to make sure that he stays that way. See, we think that maybe some person or persons made an attempt on his life. The authorities know about it, the FBI knows we're here trying to figure this out. But please, can we have your assurance that nobody needs to know about this, or that we were here asking questions?"

"Oh, sure, nobody knows anything outside of the folks you spoke to in our jam group. We'll keep it under wraps," said Bob. "Back a couple of years ago, we met Colin at a jam. He heard Barry playing a mandolin. He told us that we had a prodigy on our hands and the best thing we could do is to help him along."

Barry said, "I really wanted to play the fiddle because it plays all the melody, but all those instruments were too big. So, Colin told us about scaled down fiddles. I started with a half size and then went to three quarters. My teacher, Mrs. Ronis, says I'm learning faster than anyone she's taught." Sarah was dabbing at her eyes and Linda handed her a paper towel. "Does Colin have a keyboard he can play?"

"He does," said Fred, "and we jam every Saturday afternoon in the little store in our town. I'll tell you what, when we get back I'll have him call you and you can visit, I don't see any harm in that."

"Oh, sure," said Sarah, "that would be fine, but I wonder if you could tell us about the people he was dealing with when he came here."

Bob said, "I think Barry knows more about it than I do."

Barry began, "When he first came here he was from Indiana. He came here because he was married to a local woman. He had a delivery truck- that was his trade."

"That seems to fit," said Fred.

Barry continued, "He sold his truck and bought a mobile home for them to live in. It doesn't make sense, but he was supposed to start working for her dad who's a gulf coast engineer."

"What's that?" Sarah wanted to know.

"They build or survey or whatever anybody needs an engineering company for, but they specialize in on, or off-shore on the gulf." said Barry.

"So this guy probably had a lot of money," said Fred

"Right," said Barry. "But then, they had this falling out and Lena, that was her name, filed for divorce. He didn't contest it, but the judge decided that the mobile home was joint property so they sold it and she got half the money."

"Wow, that's a raw deal," said Fred, "but was he working for her dad?"

"No, he never did. So he had to find a job driving a truck that he didn't own, when he could have made a lot more money getting paid for himself and his truck," said Barry.

"Man, that is a very raw deal," Fred added, "So what else?"

"Colin was working for a uniform rental place. You know, garage uniforms, kitchen aprons, that sort of thing. But he needed a place to stay, and try to save up for another delivery truck. There was a pizza joint called Gino's. Gino was his buddy. Colin was delivering pizzas in the evening and night. Gino let him stay in the back of the store. That's the start of what happened to Colin. There was a court battle," said Barry.

"Well, this is just over-the-fence talk," said Bob, "we're not sure what all went on, but some, like, gang people, put the pinch on

Gino, and Colin tried to help him out. And there was a court case with lawyers and all. It wasn't something you could read about in the paper, it was kept pretty quiet. But at the end of the day, Colin left town and so did Gino. Gino sold his business and everything and went to start over somewhere else."

"Whew," said Fred, "that's the kind of thing that makes you glad you live in a small town."

"And the thing is," said Bob, "Colin, and Gino, and Gino's wife, weren't breaking any laws, they were all doing the right thing. It was these professional crooks trying to bleed people of what was rightfully theirs. So, is the FBI going to do something about this?"

"Well, look at it this way," said Fred, "They tried to do something when this all happened. Apparently, some of the gang got prosecuted and suffered fines or incarceration, but then they took out their revenge. So the FBI can try to make them pay for that, but Colin doesn't want anything to do with that. All we're doing now is trying to make sure those crooks don't come after him again."

"I can fully understand that," said Bob. "But if you all would be so kind as to ask Colin to call and talk to Barry, that's the best favor you could do for him."

"Oh, certainly," said Sarah, "I'll tell him as soon as I talk to him."

It wasn't long before Sarah spoke to Bud. She had told the musicians' group that she would call Friday morning. By seven o'clock members of ten Pine Valley families were in the store waiting for the call. Jim Tanner answered the phone. "Oh, hi Sarah. Everybody here is fine. What progress are you making?" Sarah related how they had signed up for open mic, found a jam group, met the Duncan family and a few of the things they talked about. "There's a young boy here who's dying to talk to Bud. He knew him as 'Colin' and started taking fiddle lessons at Colin's suggestion. He and his family don't know where Bud is, just that he's safe and well. Take down this number and have Bud call the little guy." She gave him the number.

"Ok," said Jim, "here's an interesting development. Kenny and Jimbo, and their friend Bobby Dumford, have pin-pointed the exact spot where Bud first landed in the creek bottom west of here before Kenny and Jimbo found him. Where the highway crosses the creek, that's where he was pushed off. Luckily he fell through some trees. That's what broke his fall."

"Amazing," said Sarah, "But I'm not so sure that information is going to help with what we're trying to do."

"But Doc told us that could be a crucial thing to know in this whole investigation," said Jim."

"Well, in any case, we'll be talking to Mr. Bishop before we decide when we're coming back. We'll let you go for now. Tell Bud to call that number and talk to Barry."

"All right, y'all be careful, now." Jim hung up. He began to fill everyone in on what Sarah had told him. "She couldn't see that what the boys had found out was useful information."

Kenny said, "Well, they could have thrown him into a lake or a river, but they didn't."

Jimbo added, "It could have been because they were just stupid and didn't pay much attention to where they were, or it could be because they didn't intend to kill him, if that makes any difference."

Bud spoke up, "It makes a difference to me, because I'm still alive and not drowned. And I'm still wondering about that twenty dollar bill."

"What twenty dollar bill?" Irene asked.

111

Jimbo said, "You remember, Mom, his billfold was empty except for one twenty dollar bill."

"Yeah," said Kenny, "and there could be some reason for it."

Arlene said, "Isn't it something, when you think about it, Bud had a group of friends down there in Texas, just like he does here, that he played music with, visited with, ate and drank with, and they're still down there wondering what the heck happened to him."

"Yeah," said Bud, "it kind of tells you something about the human race. Or, at least, our part of it. Can I use your phone, Irene?"

"Sure," she said, "But don't you want some privacy?"

"Like I need privacy? Hell, I'm happy with company." He called the number Sarah had left. The phone rang twice, then he heard, "Duncan residence, Barry speaking."

"Hey, young man, this is Colin, but you can call me, Bud. That's my name now. How's it coming on that fiddle playing?"

"Pretty good, I've learned a bunch of new songs since you saw me last."

"You've learned some new songs, that's great. I'm safe and sound here and I've got a bunch of new friends to jam with. I can't tell you where I am, but eventually we'll all get together and have a big old party. How's your mom and dad?"

"Oh, they're fine. Man, as soon as I met Fred and Sarah I've been dying to talk to you. Did you… lose all your memory?"

"Yeah, to some extent, but it's starting to come back to me, little by little. It's like, when they told me 'Barry wants to talk to you', I knew immediately who you were. Now, what are your folks' names?"

"Bob and Linda."

112

"Oh, right. You're on a small fiddle, right?"

"Yeah, three-quarters. Sarah got me a new chunk of rosin and I think I've got more bite, now. Mrs. Ronis says I'm playing as well as my dad. Can I ask you a question?"

"Sure, what's your question?"

"Do you remember having a bet on the super bowl, back in January?"

"I really don't remember, why do you ask?"

"I remember you saying that there was this guy who thought Buffalo wouldn't lose again and they wanted to bet on it. Then, you and this other guy bet against them and you won. I heard you say later that the guy hadn't paid up."

"I vaguely remember that, do you have any idea who the person was?"

"I don't know what his name was."

"Tell you what, Barry, I'll think on that, it may be a connection to what got me abducted by the gangsters. Say, there's somebody here that needs to talk to you. He's an FBI agent and his name is Pete Bishop. He's in charge of my case and you can trust him. First tell your parents that you're going to talk to him, ok?"

Barry told his parents, "I'm going to talk to an FBI agent that's in charge of Colin's case."

"Hello, Barry?"

"Yep, I'm here," said Barry.

"Ok, other than what you've told Fred and Sarah, and Colin, is there anything else you know of, that might tell us something about friends or acquaintances of his?"

Barry paused, "Like Gino, maybe?"

"Uh, yeah, we could start there."

"Well, Gino moved away with his business. He and his wife took

113

everything they had and moved to Missouri. Gino came from Naples. He had to be somewhere where there were no Italians. He would be away from the Texas gang as well."

"I see, where did you hear all this, if you don't mind my asking?" said Mr. Bishop.

"Mostly at the barber shop. We go to a barber shop called Luigi's. When you're just a kid they don't think you know what they're talking about." Barry explained. "So he wouldn't be in St. Louis and he wouldn't be in Kansas City, but somewhere else."

"I see. Well, let me put your friend back on here. Thanks, you've been good help." He handed the phone back to Bud.

Bud said, "I'll say goodbye for now, but I've got your number, so I'll call back sometime."

Barry said, "Ok, I'm just so glad you're safe and healthy. Bye, Colin."

Agent Bishop was back in his office when Fred called. "Hello, Pete Bishop."

"Hey Pete, this is Fred. Sarah and I are still in Texas. We're calling about what we found out."

"I spoke with Barry Duncan, that is one amazing kid," said Pete. "Is there anybody in particular you need to talk to some more before you come back?"

"I don't think so. We'd have to dig up somebody else besides who we've talked to already."

"Oh, all right, in that case, come on back to Pine Valley and we'll get our drop-in and you guys together. I'll come down and we'll see what we've got to work with, ok?"

Fred said, "All right, we'll do that, I'll call you when we get back."

The phone rang again, it was Bud. "Hello Pete, it's me, Bud."

"Yeah, what's happening?"

"I just wanted to tell you the rest of what Barry told me.

"And what did he have to say?"

"Well, among other things, he knew something about what went on down there when my divorce was happening."

"Do me a favor, Bud," said Mr. Bishop.

"What's that?" Bud replied.

"Write all that down, and when Fred and Sarah get back, we'll sit down together and talk about it."

Chapter 14

It was just past mid-day and Bud and Arlene were on their way to Texarkana to pick up Sarah and Fred. Bud was driving Arlene's pickup. "You know it's funny about memory," said Bud, "you can forget how to spell cat, but you can't forget how to drive."

"That's because it's muscle memory," Arlene replied, "I guess it's in your brain, but it's mostly the rest of your nervous system."

"I guess they could program a robot to drive a car," said Bud.

"That's a scary thought," Arlene said, "I wouldn't want to ride with one. Tell me something."

Bud said, "Ok what's that?"

"Have you ever seen a church called, 'St. John the Baptist Catholic Church?"

"Yeah when I was a kid there was a church with that name in my neighborhood." Bud replied.

Arlene said, "So, you think somewhere there might be a St. John the Catholic Baptist Church?"

Bud laughed, "It would be funny to put up a sign to watch people's reaction."

As soon as they pulled into the parking lot of the car rental place, Fred emerged from the door with Sarah close behind. "So how is the espionage business?" Arlene inquired.

"Not too bad for a couple of days but I wouldn't do it as a full-time job," Sarah replied. "Actually we met some real nice folks. Have you all eaten lunch yet?"

Arlene said, "No we haven't, if you want to stop at Bryce's, I'll pop for it."

"What's Bryce's?" Bud asked.

"Oh, yeah, you're new around here. It's about the best cafeteria you've ever been to. Their pecan pie is to die for." Arlene explained.

Fred and Sarah both agreed. Bryce's had its own exit sign off I-thirty.

Fred said, "Don't be fooled by what the fried chicken looks like, it's way better than what you get at Church's."

Sarah said, "If nobody minds, I'm through with driving for a few days."

"You all didn't drive on the interstate?" Bud asked.

"No, but once we got close to Houston it was all freeway," said Sarah,

"and those people don't drive like we do in Arkansas."

Everyone put a piece of pecan pie on their tray. Arlene picked up the check but Bud gave two bucks to the waiter who carried the ladies' trays.

"We used to call this Karo nut pie at home," said Arlene. Bud looked quizzical, so Arlene explained. "The original recipe came from the Karo syrup label. But this stuff, is kind of a cross between Karo nut and custard."

"I think they perfected it," said Fred.

"You know, it's funny," said Bud, "I don't remember a lot of things, but I'm pretty sure I never ate better food than this in my life."

Bud pulled onto I-thirty with the intention of going north on US seventy-one. They had only gone a couple of miles when they came upon a tractor-trailer rig parked on the shoulder with its emergency flashers turned on. Bud said, "I'm going to stop, that driver might need help." He pulled off the highway, then ran back to the eighteen-wheeler. He climbed up on the running board and peered in the window which was rolled down. There was woman sitting in the shotgun seat. The man in the driver's seat was lying with his head in the woman's lap. "Do you folks need help?" Bud asked.

The woman said, "My husband was driving, when all of a

117

sudden he got this abdominal pain, really strong. I can't imagine what's wrong."

"It's his belly, not his chest?" Bud inquired. She nodded. "Well, he needs to see a doctor," Bud opined, "Where were you heading?"

"To the Wal-Mart in Little Rock," she replied.

"Is this their rig?" asked Bud.

"No, it's ours. We're supposed to be there by this evening," she replied.

"Wait just a second while I confer with my colleagues. I think we may be able to help you out," said Bud. He trotted back to the pickup. "This guy all of a sudden got a serious bellyache. He and his wife were headed to Little Rock and they were expected by tonight. If Fred and Sarah could take them to a doctor, Arlene and I could drive his rig to Little Rock."

Sarah said, "We can just take him to the ER at St. Michael's in Texarkana, it wouldn't take but five minutes."

"All right, I'll back up the pickup, and we'll load him up," said Bud.

Bud went back to the truck. "Ma'am, my partner and I can drive your rig to Little Rock. Our friends can drive you and your husband to the emergency room. Would that be all right?"

"Oh, lord, thank you so much. That would be the best thing you could do" she replied.

"Let's get your husband in the pickup and we'll be on our way in a second," said Bud.

While they were situating the man, Bud talked to the woman. She said, "Here's the keys, take I-four thirty north, go west on Financial Center Parkway to Bowman Road, you'll see it from there."

Bud told Fred to call Maggie and tell her to find out where they needed to bring the truck when they came back. He said, "When I get to Little Rock, I'll call Maggie to find out where they'll be."

The couple's names were Bill and Halley German. They were late middle aged and went together on runs, but Halley didn't drive. She was usually the navigator.

"I didn't know Bud could drive a big rig," Sarah commented.

"I didn't either, until now," Fred replied, "You folks just happened upon a rare individual. He showed up in our little town right out of thin air and found a new home. But we can't tell anymore about him, except that he's a very talented man."

"Sounds really intriguing," Halley commented, "I have a feeling this will all work out and it's really a blessing."

By the time they reached St. Michael's, Bill's pain had subsided but he still needed to see a doctor to find out what was happening. They took Bill into an examining room. He sat on the bed and Halley sat in a chair by the door. A woman with a clip board came in. She said, "The doctor will be here in a moment. May I ask you some questions?"

Bill said, "Yes."

She got his name and age and the name of his insurance company. Then the doctor came in.

"I'm Dr. Wren," he said, "you were having pain?"

"Yes, sharp pain, like I got kicked by a mule."

"Whereabouts?" Bill pointed to his lower abdomen. "Lie back please," said the doctor. Bill laid on the bed and the doctor began to probe to find the source of the pain. He couldn't find a spot that was sensitive. "Have you had this pain before?"

Bill said, "Maybe once before. It lasted a minute or two, then went away."

"Has anyone in your family ever had a gall bladder problem?"

"I think my grandmother did."

"Where do you live, Mr. German?"

"In Fort Worth. I was on my way to Little Rock in my eighteen-wheeler when this happened. Another driver offered to make the run for me, so I'm just going to stay here 'til he gets back."

"I see. I've a suspicion that it's your gall bladder, but we'd need to do a sonogram to confirm it. I could schedule one for you tomorrow morning in x-ray. Would you like for me to do that?" the doctor asked.

Bill said, "I don't see why not if I'm going to be here anyway."

The doctor said, "Take a seat right outside this door and I'll have a nurse set that up for you. Now, if the sonogram shows that you have gallstones, they likely caused a blockage of the bile duct, and that would be the cause of the pain. When you get back home, you need to show the films to your doctor so he can decide if you need surgery."

Bill said "Thank you doctor," as Dr. Wren left. Bill and Halley sat in two chairs outside the examining room. A nurse led them to an office where another woman got more information about Bill and then scheduled them for an appointment at ten AM in the x-ray department. They left the ER into the main hospital corridor. Fred and Sarah were waiting just a short way down the hall. Bill told them that he was staying overnight to get his sonogram and waiting for Bud to bring his truck back.

"Well," said Sarah, "Do you need a place to stay? We live in Pine Valley, it's about forty miles from here."

"Oh, no, you folks have done enough, we'll be all right. We'll spend the night at the Comfort Suites on I-thirty west. Now we just need to rent a car."

"Rent a car?" asked Fred, with a laugh, "We know just the place. C'mon, we'll drive you there."

When Bud and Arlene both had their seat belts fastened, Bud eased the big rig onto I-thirty. "You're familiar with this territory?" Bud asked.

"Pretty much," Arlene replied. "Just stay on this route for the next hundred miles or so 'til we run into four thirty. Then north. Where's the gearshift on this thing?"

"It's an automatic, lots easier than a stick. You can give all your attention to just being ready to slow down or change lanes." Bud replied. "Write down 'Financial Center, and Bowman Road.'"

"Got it already. So you've driven one of these before?"

"I guess I have. Didn't have any nagging feeling like, are you sure you can do this. I just knew, somehow, that I could do it."

"Well, Mr. German trusted you. You didn't tell him you'd had amnesia did you?"

"Nah, I guess if a guy shows up and says, 'Do you want me to drive this thing for you?' You don't ask a lot of questions. I guess I could have told him I don't even know who I am."

Arlene laughed. "You know, if you decide you want to do this on a regular basis, I'd be willing to quit my caretaking job and ride with you."

Bud glanced over at her. He didn't say anything for several seconds.

"But you love that job. You mean, you're worried about me taking off to drive trucks? Hell no, I'm gonna stay in Pine Valley until they run me off. Can you deal with that?"

Arlene's eyes were starting to tear up. She said, "Yeah, I can deal with that. Thanks Bud."

There was considerable traffic on I-thirty but it didn't seem crowded.

"I wouldn't mind any hints you feel like might help. I can't really remember how good my instincts are," said Bud.

Arlene said, "There are quite a few exits between here and Little Rock. The next sizable one is Arkadelphia. At Malvern, which is

121

about half way, there's a pretty large rest area which is in the center of the eastbound and westbound lanes. So it would be an exit to the left."

Bud said, "I'll keep that in mind. I might feel inclined to take a little break by then."

Another twenty miles went by and they were approaching the Hope exit. Bud asked, "Hope, where did I hear about that?"

"It's the president's home town. Although he graduated from Hot Springs High." Arlene replied.

"Oh yeah, I remember now. You know, driving this rig down this interstate is kind of jogging my memory, to a certain extent." said Bud.

"You could, while we're traveling, kind of tell me what goes through your mind. If it won't distract from your driving," Arlene commented.

"Oh, no, it might even help keep me focused. Ok, for one thing, truck stops will have prominent signs, well in advance of the exits. Along with them will be a variety of food places. And also places like Walmart because a trucker needs a few supplies, and the convenience stores are way too high priced. You may have noticed, only rarely do big oil company stations carry diesel. When they do, it's always on interstates. If a trucker gets in a bind, he can always just put gas in his tank- just enough to get him to the next place he can get diesel."

Arlene asked, "How's our fuel supply?"

"It's fine for the time being. By the time we unload in Little Rock, we'll need to refuel before we head back," was Bud's reply.

"It seems like it takes a level headed person to do this work," Arlene suggested.

Bud said, "Yeah, they don't do any drag racing, or passing on the right, or anything but cooperation. The worst thing is the guys who take pills to stay awake."

122

"I thought they had gotten that under control."

"Well, they tried, but I don't think they got anywhere. I knew a guy who used to drive Mexican steers from south of the border to rodeo companies. He would take a piece of iron pipe with caps on both ends. Fill it up with pills and throw it in the manure in the bed of the truck with the steers. What border patrol was going to crawl around in that cow shit looking for contraband?" Bud related.

Arlene chuckled, "No, I guess they wouldn't."

Chapter 15

Gino was closing his little restaurant for the night. It was ten pm and, he had made only a dozen pizzas since noon. He had talked to Colin on the phone every week or so since they'd first made contact. They wanted to visit, but they had never found the time. He had tried to call Colin that morning but got an error message. He said to Millie, "I don't understand what could have happened to Colin. We've both called that number he left and they said the number wasn't working. Are you sure you didn't get a call telling us he'd moved?"

"No it's been the same since he's been there," Millie replied, "the number must have changed for some reason."

"I'm going to call the FBI and see if they can tell me something," said Gino. "It will at least be better than just wondering about it."

On Monday he called the FBI office in Kansas. A woman took down his name and phone number and Colin's name. In the late afternoon the phone rang. When Gino answered, a man asked, "Is this Gino Candiota?"

"Yes it is, I was calling about a friend named Colin Rayburn, who went in a witness protection program and was relocated," said Gino.

"Ok, I've found the case you were asking about. The agent who is in charge of that case is in another state. I've forwarded your case to him and he should be contacting you in the next few days with regard to your friend. Now I can tell you this. The person you referred to is no longer in Kansas. He's in another state, but he's in no danger. The agent in charge of his case is in contact with him. As I said, he will contact you in the next couple of days with information about your friend."

Gino breathed a sigh of relief. He said, "Oh, you don't know how relieved I am to hear you say that." He smiled at Millie.

The agent said, "Is there anything else I can help you with?"

"No, that's fine," said Gino, "I'll wait for the call." He hung up the phone and embraced his wife. "He's not in Kansas anymore, they've moved him somewhere else but he's fine. The FBI agent who's in charge of his case will call us in a few days and tell us more. But we don't need to worry, he's safe where he is."

Millie said, "I'm so relieved to hear that. I was beginning to think those Starr people got ahold of him again. Well, let's go home, I think I can sleep a lot better now."

Pete Bishop called on Tuesday morning. Gino answered the phone. "Gino's Pizza, may I help you."

"Hi. Gino, this is Pete Bishop with the FBI. You were checking on one of our contacts?"

"Oh, yes, our friend Colin, I'm not sure what his name is now. We had his phone number, but then he didn't answer when I tried to call him."

"I'm sorry to hear that, Gino. Yes, we had him relocated," said Mr. Bishop, "but somehow his enemies slipped under the radar, and we think they tried to get rid of him. Fortunately they didn't succeed and he's in a new location now. I'm currently the only agent on his case. I'll ask him to call you, but I can't give you his phone number. And, rest assured, he's safe where he is. I guess you could say he's found a new home. Now, are you the folks that left Texas about the same time he did?"

"That would be me and my wife, Millie," said Gino. "We've got a new place now, and things are going along pretty well."

"Well, I won't keep you long. One of these days we'll get past all this secrecy and life will be back to normal."

"Thank you Mr. Bishop," said Gino. "Tell him we're right here when he gets a chance to call. He'll know the best time to call, he's worked for me before."

Bishop said, "Thanks for your help, I'll be in touch."

125

Before they left St. Michael's, Fred called Maggie to fill her in on what was happening. As soon as she knew it was Fred on the phone Maggie asked, "Where are you?"

Fred said, "First let me assure that I'm fine. Sarah's fine. Bud and Arlene are on their way to Little Rock via I-thirty, I'll explain that in a minute. Sarah and I are at St. Michael's Hospital in Texarkana. We brought somebody here who needed medical attention, and as soon as we talk to them and get them situated we'll be coming back."

Maggie said, "I'm sure there's a logical explanation for all this, but how can Bud and Arlene be going to Little Rock?"

"Oh, well, we happened upon this truck driver with a severe belly ache. He needed medical attention and his truckload of merchandise needed to get to Little Rock and so Bud volunteered to drive it there," Fred explained. There was a long pause.

"You're not putting me on, are you?" Maggie commented.

"No, I know it's hard to believe," Fred replied, "maybe this is why people decide to write books. I don't know. Could you call any interested parties and pass along the information?"

"Oh, I will, but I think I might lie and say it was car trouble."

Fred said, "Now Bud will call to find out where to bring the truck. The couple, Bill and Halley, will be at the Comfort Suites on the right heading west, just outside Texarkana. Have you got that?"

"Comfort suites on I-thirty west on the right. I've got it. How soon are you leaving there?"

"I'm taking them to rent a car right now. As soon as I do that we're heading back," said Fred. "I'll see you when I get back."

When Bud and Arlene found the Walmart, they knew the loading docks would be on the opposite side from the entrance. Bud didn't have any trouble finding his way there. There was a

126

Sam's Club store right next to the Walmart and he hoped that all his load was destined for Walmart. As he approached the loading dock a man in a uniform came walking towards him. He rolled down the window and held out the clipboard, which the man took from him. "Mr. German?" the man said.

"No, I'm um..."

Arlene said, "Mr. Russell."

"Mr. Russell. Mr. German had a medical emergency at the last moment and I had to fill in for him."

"Oh, yes, I see here that Mr. German called and said you'd be filling in. What are your names?"

"Bud and Arlene," Bud replied.

"Fine, back up to that bay on the end and we'll get you unloaded."

Bud pulled away from the building a little and proceeded to back the rig to the loading dock. When he was almost there Arlene said, "Now I'm certain that you've had experience driving an eighteen wheeler."

When Bud had the trailer flush with the end of the dock he said, "Well I don't know, it could just be beginner's luck. If there is such a thing."

"But still no certain memory about where or when?" Arlene asked.

"No, not for certain, but if it does come to me, it'll be you who helped me find it. Just coming up here with me helped a lot. I never had a chance to start worrying about what I was doing." Bud paused, "Now we need to call Maggie and find out where to go."

"Why don't you stay here in case they need you to move somewhere," Arlene suggested, "I'll go in and call."

"Good idea," Bud replied.

Arlene entered a door with a sign that read 'office.' They let her make a collect call. Maggie answered on the second ring. "Hi, Fred's place."

"Hi, Maggie, it's Arlene."

"Oh, hi. Don't tell me you're in Little Rock," said Maggie.

"As a matter of fact we are. We're in back of the Walmart getting this tractor trailer unloaded," Arlene replied.

"Well, the message is, the truck needs to go to the Comfort Suites on the right side of I-thirty, going west, outside Texarkana. So, apparently, Bud can drive a big rig." said Maggie.

"Well, nobody thought to ask him if he *could* do it, he just did."

"So what's the plan?" Maggie asked.

"Well, we'll grab a bite to eat and then head back…oh, I guess it might help if somebody would meet us when we get to the motel in Texarkana." Arlene added.

"What time?" Maggie asked

"Oh, there's got to be a way to figure this. I know, we'll call when we get to Arkadelphia. If somebody left Pine Valley right after that, it should be, sort of, close to the right time. If somebody has to wait a few minutes it won't be a big deal." Arlene concluded.

Maggie said, "All right, call from Arkadelphia. See you later."

Arlene found Bud waiting in the truck when she left the office. Bud said, "What's the scoop?"

"Halley and Bill will be at the Comfort Suites, on the right hand side of I-thirty, going west, outside of Texarkana. We'll stop in Arkadelphia and call. Somebody will leave Pine Valley at that time to come pick us up," Arlene related.

"Sounds fine. You know Arlene, you're a winner," Bud replied. "Want to try driving this truck?"

"Well, maybe when we get to Clark county," Arlene replied. "I don't have a chauffer's license, if that makes a difference."

"I hadn't thought of that," Bud replied. "Well, for the most part, what you would learn the most about, is putting the brakes on soon enough to make a smooth stop."

Arlene said, "Oh yeah, I've heard about those emergency stops they

128

have in the mountains when they get to coasting too fast downhill."

"Yeah, never used one of those…well I don't remember using one," said Bud.

"Well, I've got a question. They have those signs in small towns that say, 'no jake brakes.' What the heck does that mean?" asked Arlene

Bud said, "You can slow a vehicle down, with a gas engine, by using compression, you know, shift to a lower gear and let out the clutch. Well diesel engines don't have spark plugs or valves, so that doesn't work unless you have jake brakes. They were first made by the Jacobs brake company. What they do is let the compression off the combustion chamber which slows the engine and the truck. The sound they make is like a jackhammer, only much louder."

"Oh yeah, I've heard that sound before." said Arlene.

Bud said, "Now I've got a question for you. How come there's no black people around Pine Valley?"

"Well, in this part of Arkansas, towns never had a white section and a black section. There are towns that are nearly all black, like Antoine, Tollette, Clow, and Schaal."

"I see. And they've got their own businesses?"

"Yeah, but there's a certain amount of interaction."

Then Arlene said, "Say, why don't we stop at the rest stop just south of Malvern? We don't need gas but there's plenty of space there."

Bud said, "That's ok by me, but it's not gas, we don't need, it's diesel we don't need."

"All right, I stand corrected."

When they got to the rest stop Arlene volunteered to make the phone call. Maggie answered the phone. "Hey, said Arlene, "it's your emergency truck drivers here. Now, we're at the rest stop south of Malvern, so figure on that much time 'til we hit T-town."

"I read you Miss Amonette. The jam group has a surprise for Bud next Saturday. It's a secret so I can't tell you. Fred is all cranked up to pick you up, so I'll let him know."

"Thanks, Maggie, I'll see you when you get here. Bye, now."

Fred was there waiting at the motel when Bud and Arlene rolled in.

They bid goodbye to Bill and Halley and wished them luck. Bill asked them what he could do to repay them. Arlene told them to do a favor for some travelers the next chance they got.

Fred was driving as they headed back to Pine Valley. Nobody spoke for several minutes. Curiosity was getting to Bud and he finally said, "So what's this surprise Maggie was talking about?"

Fred said, "Well, it was supposed to be a secret until Saturday, but we figured that since you were supposed to participate in creating it, we've got to let you in on it."

"I don't have a clue as to what it might be," said Bud, "Pull my coat,"

Fred said, "All right, it goes like this. 'When I first came to Pine Valley, I was a man without a name. Didn't know where I was going, or the place from where I came.' And that's as far as we got."

Bud said, "O lord, you expect me to follow that up?"

"Well, it's just like a jigsaw puzzle, you keep on hunting 'til you find the next piece," Fred told him.

Arlene said, "Sure, you just set it aside in some corner of your brain, and when the right line comes along, you'll know it."

"It's to the tune of 'When First Unto this Country a Stranger I Came'," Fred explained.

Bud said, "Ok, how about: 'They took me in and fed me, and made me feel at home."

Arlene said, "Huh, we need two lines, and the second one rhymes with 'home."

"This woman's amazing," said Bud.

Arlene said, "That meter doesn't fit."

Everyone was silent for several minutes, then Fred said, "Well, the story's still unfolding, the rest we'll leave for later. Anyone have a pen?"

Bud said, "I just remembered."

"You just remembered what?" Arlene asked.

"Back when I first got my truck, I couldn't get a chauffer's license without taking drivers training. And in drivers training I drove all the different trucks there are."

"And you drove eighteen wheelers," said Arlene.

"Every day for about a week." said Bud.

Chapter 16

Pete Bishop had information from the Houston area musicians. He had information from the FBI's Kansas office. He had been in fairly close contact with the people of Pine Valley. He had notified his superiors that he thought they should send an agent into the Houston area to investigate illegal activities by the group who had targeted Colin Rayburn- probably Starline. The man that was assigned the job was named Cody Carlton.

Cody had earned his bachelor's in political science from LSU. He had light brown hair and was five feet eight inches tall. In his senior year he spoke with a handful of recruiters about jobs. He figured that for the legal system to function there had to be enforcement and he had always had an interest in federal law. He had thought about going to law school, but the recruiter said the FBI would teach him a lot about the law and he could be earning a paycheck while he was in training. He got married. When he was twenty-seven he became a field agent and got sent to Arkansas. They figured since he was from Louisiana he could understand the accent, but they all really sounded like hicks to him- even the ones running businesses.

Cody had a local agent, a woman named Roxanne Savage, assigned to assist him. The name she went by was Rocky. She couldn't be described as pretty, just sort of plain, but Cody thought she had sex appeal. She was a little bit older than he was and she was about his height and size. She told him to meet her at the Purple Door. She was sitting in a booth drinking a beer when he came in the door.

"You must Rocky," he said as he approached.

"You must be Cody," she replied. "You want a drink?"

"Yeah, let me get a Sprite, I'll be right back."

The first thing she said as he sat down was, "I'll tell you about this kid Barry Duncan, he's got a tape recorder memory. He remembers every conservation he hears, just like he remembers tunes that he plays on his fiddle."

"Sounds awesome, he'd make a great agent," Cody remarked, "but he could make more money playing his fiddle."

"Tell me about it. But just by hanging around Luigi's barber shop he learned about several things we can check on."

"I see," said Cody, "But fill me in on this gang they were working on."

"The main guy is Starr, but he's much too well greased to get a grip on. His manager was Buskirk, although he may have gotten demoted since then. Rayburn testified against him for labor violations and he got popped for six months and fifty grand."

"Is that why they retaliated against him?"

"Apparently. They really got outside the playground on that one."

"Yeah, they did. But here's the deal, the agency wants us to find out who took the assignment so they can offer them a deal. Like 'either we pop you for attempted murder or you tell us what you know about the boss'," Cody explained. "Of course, we aren't the people who get to decide where and when that's going to happen. We just interview this list of people to find whatever info they need to complete the jig-saw puzzle."

Rocky said, "So, where do we start? Do we go talk to the genius kid?"

"That's as good a place to start as anywhere else, "said Cody.

At the Duncan residence Barry was home from school and his mother was in the kitchen when the phone rang. Linda answered it. "Hello, this is Linda."

Rocky said, "Hi, this is Roxanne Savage, I'm an agent for the FBI. We're trying to get some background on Colin Rayburn and I understand that you folks knew him."

"Ah, yes we do, but I thought he was in a safe place." said Linda.

"Yes, as a matter of fact he is. What we're doing is trying to find out why and how these local crooks tried to do him in. But see, we're not going to involve him in this. As far as we're concerned, any connection he had with them is water under the bridge. We're just doing what we can to make south Texas a better and safer place to live," Rocky explained.

"Ok," said Mrs. Duncan, "my husband, Bob will be home within the hour, why don't you drop by around six."

"That's fine," said Rocky, "my partner, Cody Carlton, and I'll be there then, goodbye."

When Bob Duncan came home his son Barry told him about the two

132

FBI agents that would be dropping by. Bob said, "If these people are FBI, who were those other people?"

Barry explained, "They were just people that knew Colin when he showed up in their town unexpectedly."

Mrs. Duncan came in and sat down with Bob and Barry. She said, "I heard what you all were saying about Fred and Sarah. Apparently they just volunteered to come here looking for people that knew Colin. It gives you the feeling that he's a very likable person to have friends who'd go out of their way to help him."

Cody and Rocky soon arrived. After greeting the Duncans they got down to business. Cody said, "I want to be clear about this, Mr. Rayburn is no longer involved in this process. He's safe and happy where he is. We won't take up a lot of your time, we're just interested in the folks we refer to as the south Texas mob. Barry, can you tell us where you got your information about the Starr people?"

"At Luigi's barber shop," said Barry, "A guy named Curley comes in there on Saturdays. If anybody wants to bet on games he takes their bet."

Bob asked, "Now is any of this about appearing in court at some time?"

"No." said Rocky, "You folks won't be involved in any legal proceeding. We're just looking for people connected with these illegal activities. They're the ones who'll be involved in the court cases."

"You folks have done more than your share of helping us. The only thing we ask is if anyone asks you about any of this, just say you don't know anything about it," said Cody.

"Ok, that's fine," said Bob. "Barry, is there anybody else you know about?"

"All I know is there are more people that go around to different places and take bets, but I don't know who they are. But I've heard about a place called the 'Sportsman' where they have three or four TV sets with different games on. People make bets there all the time, but I don't know who their betting guy is."

"Well, we'll get out of your hair," said Cody, "We want to thank you folks so much for helping us. Like I said, we're just trying to make this community a safer place to live."

133

As they were getting up Rocky said, "Good luck with your music playing, you folks are really blest to have a young man like this to play for other people."

When the agents left Linda went back to the kitchen to fix supper. Barry said, "Dad, I don't see why it's so important about the gambling."

Bob said, "Well see, for example, if two guys just bet on a game between themselves it's just them winning or losing. But these professional guys, they know what the odds are and they don't usually lose bets. They lose every once in a while just to make it look like they're on the up and up. But over a period of time they make a lot of money. It's not just those guys like Curley. He gets paid by the big boys who are running the whole thing. At race tracks and casinos and lotteries you usually lose there as well, but the state gets a lot of tax money out of it. These local professionals don't pay taxes, and, if I'm not mistaken, they launder that money through small time business so they can make it look like that money never changed hands."

"Wow," said Barry, "I never realized crime was so complicated."

The next place Cody and Rocky went to was the Sportsman.

Rocky said, "Well, we've got the name of one club, and the name of one person, but we've got to start somewhere."

The Sportsman was next to an on ramp on the freeway. It had a big parking lot and five TV sets, so if there was ever a time that five different games were on, the Sportsman was the place to be. Baseball in the summer, football in the fall, basketball and hockey in the winter. Then there was the NCAA as opposed to the pros. Americans have lots of sports to bet on. And some folks can't watch a game without wanting to bet.

Cody and Rocky took a seat at the bar. When the bartender came over, Cody said, "Draw a Bud for her and a Sprite for me." When they got their drinks they just sat there for a few minutes without saying anything. On the fifty inch screen in back of the bar they were showing highlights of the Denver Broncos last season. It was kind of strange that Wade Phillips was a Denver coach right after Dan Reeves. Texas seemed to have a certain influence on Colorado.

Rocky ordered a refill, and when the bartender came with their drinks, Cody nonchalantly asked, "How could a guy put down a bet on a game around here?"

The bartender said, "Oh, well, there's a guy named Tinsley that comes in here a lot. He covers just about anybody's bet and he's pretty lucky. He wins most of the time."

"That so," said Cody, "I'm not big on baseball but I'm pretty good on football, I'll check him out. And your name is?"

The bartender said, "Aaron."

"I'm Carl and this is Sandy. See you around." said Cody.

When they were back in the car Rocky said, "What's next?"

"I guess Pandora's," Cody replied. "I got the name 'Carl' from that John Prine song where he says, 'she called everybody Carl."

"I guess I'll have to remember to answer to Sandy," said Rocky. "Let me write a few things down before we go to Pandora's."

Pandora's had a relatively modern atmosphere. It seemed to appeal to a younger clientele. As they entered the place Rocky said, "Hey, do you want to change roles this time?"

"You mean I'll drink beer and you drink Sprite?" Cody asked, "Or become gay."

Rocky said, "I was never very good at acting. But, as a matter of fact, I think I'll drink something non-alcoholic. Too many drinks and you forget what you're here for." There were four TV screens. They sat at the bar and ordered a Sprite and a Kaliber. The bartender's name was Rex. When Rocky asked about betting Rex said, "Oh, I suppose this guy named Nicholls will cover a bet on most things. He's in here on weekends and a few other days."

Cody took notice of the fact that there were three young women sitting together in one of the booths, and when a few men wandered in, the girls split up and each one went over to talk to one of the men. He leaned over to Rocky, "You see those girls?"

"Yeah, they're hookers. There's a lot of money in that business, but we don't waste time on it. Where to next?"

"Starbucks."

135

When they got to the place Rocky said, "This doesn't look like a bar."

"It's not," Cody replied, "it's a coffeehouse." They stood in line and put in their orders. Rocky ordered an espresso and a long john. Cody ordered a latte. They sat in a small table back in a corner.

"Wow," said Rocky, "So this place is where a racket is going on? No booze, no drugs, no games."

"Yeah, well, coffee is a legal version of speed, and, with the popularity of the stuff, there are millions of people in these places you wouldn't connect with in those other places." Cody explained. "Oh, wait, there's a TV set over by the restrooms. What's it got on?"

"Looks like a tennis match," Rocky replied. "That seems to fit. I think I'll go hang out over there a few minutes." Rocky tried to look like she was standing in line. When a barrista came by she asked, "Hi, I'm Sandy. Does anybody bet on these tennis matches?"

"Oh sure, I'll cover whatever player you want to bet on. My name's Penny, I've been working here since it opened." said the woman.

"Great" Rocky responded, "I like to watch the women's matches."

Rocky looked around and saw Cody standing by the window. When she walked over he said, "I'm kind of hungry, you want to get something to eat?" Rocky nodded. "What do they have for Mexican around here?"

Rocky said, "Tia Maria's is pretty good if you like Tex-Mex."

"Sounds good," said Cody, "Do they sell alcohol?"

"Fifty-seven kinds of tequila and mescal."

"All right, let's check it out." As they were driving across town Cody said, "I gotta tell you about something my wife said one time. We were checking out this new Tex-Mex place. When we were ordering, my wife ordered a fruit salad. Then they brought our food but not the fruit salad. So I asked the waiter, 'what about the fruit salad?' He went to check. When he came back he said, 'Senor, they are still chopping the fruit.' I said, 'Ok.' Then my wife says, 'Did he say they were still shopping for the fruit?'"

"How funny," said Rocky.

"Yeah, I can never tell that around her, she can't live it down. You know how when Hispanic people say 'chop' it comes out 'shop'."

"Yeah, this place we're going to, if you ask them a question about anything they send another wait person to talk to you. I can understand it, learning a new language takes a lot of time. My old man used to say that everybody should work in a restaurant some time or other just to feel what it's like working for tips. Well, here's the place."

"You want something to drink?" the waitress asked.

Cody ordered a Dos Equis and Rocky ordered a margarita. "You know where the name 'margarita' comes from?" Cody asked.

"Yeah, it means 'daisy' in some language." Rocky replied.

"Right, Margarita is the Spanish name for Daisy."

"I always wondered why we hear so many Cajun jokes in east Texas," said Rocky.

"Well, I guess we need a subculture to tell jokes about, and Cajuns don't seem to mind. We've got some comedians that made a career of it, like Justin Wilson and JB Kling. Have you heard any good ones?" Cody inquired.

"One that sticks in my head goes like this. A teenage girl comes home and her mom asks her how she's doing. She tells her mom she thinks she's pregnant. Her mom says, 'Now calm down, honey, let's think about it. Are you sure it's yours?'"

"Never heard that one." said Cody, "that's pretty good. But that could be a joke in many different subcultures."

When the waitress returned Cody ordered some rellenos and Rocky ordered a burrito.

When the waitress left Cody said, "I wonder if gambling goes on in a place like this."

"Probably so," said Rocky, "but they might have their own in-house bookie, and it's only among Spanish speaking people."

"I forgot something," Cody interjected.

"You forgot what?" said Rocky.

"Something I was supposed to be doing. Any of these places we were going to, we were supposed to be asking about uniform and linen service." Cody replied. "It's one of the businesses Starr was involved in."

"Well, we've had the barber shop, Sportsman's, Pandora's, and

137

Starbucks. I guess any of them could use the service. But wouldn't it seem a little bit awkward asking about uniforms and gambling at the same time?" Rocky observed."

"Yeah, it would, maybe that's why I didn't think about it before." said Cody. "I've got an idea, we could just get on the phone and pretend we're a new company and ask if they need linens and uniforms."

So, it was over to Rocky's place. Cody sat back on the sofa and set the phone in his lap while Rocky brewed a pot of coffee. They started through the restaurant and club listings in the yellow pages. The conversation was, "Do you need somebody to handle your napkins and aprons?" After calling a dozen places they found out that most of them used South Texas for their service. Then they called the Tia Maria's. Cody asked, "Who handles your napkins and aprons?"

The answer was, "A guy named Ronnie. Oh, you mean the company? I gotta ask. 'Octavio, who does our aprons and stuff? He says it's South Texas Laundry Service."

"Thanks amigo," said Cody. He was shaking his head but smiling.

Rocky asked, "You found something out, didn't you."

"Yeah, get this," said Cody, "they said they use South Texas Laundry and the deliveryman was a guy named Ronnie. Pete Bishop was looking for somebody named Ronnie that made a bet with Colin."
"What's his last name?" Rocky asked.

"I don't know but we've got to find out. We've got a first name and we need a last name. We know he works for South Texas Laundry," said Cody.

"Let's get the agency to find out what the name is. They can use the IRS to find out his name," said Rocky. "He might be just the man we're looking for. We'll call Pete Bishop."

Pete Bishop answered on the second ring, "Bishop."

"Yeah, this is Cody Carlton down in Houston. I think we might have found somebody you're looking for. We were talking to people at these clubs and such. A guy at this Mexican restaurant told us the guy who delivers their napkins and aprons is named Ronnie. It's the same company Colin worked for- South Texas Laundry Service. Don't know

138

his last name but you should be able to find him."

Pete said, "Yeah, if he works for that company he knew Colin. We'll get an ID on him. He might be exactly the guy we're looking for. Nice works, guys. What else have you got?"

Cody said, "So far we've gone to nine or ten places. Clubs, a coffee shop, a barber shop, and a couple of restaurants we've been to altogether. We've got contact names on most of them."

"Well, keep me posted when you can, make a report to hand in. I'll get a last name on your guy, Ronnie," said Bishop.

"Yeah, let us know on that one, I'm curious about that. Talk to you later," said Cody.

The jam that Saturday was at Irene's store. The Tanners were there, along with Fred, Maggie, Sarah, Ace, Kate, Ruth, Dexter, Charles, Bud and Arlene. They were tuning up when Fred said, "I've been thinking."

Jim said, "Oh, no."

"Well listen, you might be interested. First we can give ourselves a name. I was thinking maybe the Pine Valley Drifters. All the local nursing homes like to have people come play music. We just print up a flyer- we'll play for free or they can pay us for gas money. If somebody's having a surprise party we can ask for a donation. There are eight or nine of us in the group. If anybody can't make it, it's ok since we've got enough people to make a good group. What do you all think?"

Maggie said, "I really don't think anybody would have a problem with that. If it's free, who's going to complain?"

Bud said, "Pine Valley Drifters sounds like a fine name to me. If we just have two or three phone numbers on the flyer they're bound to connect with somebody."

Ace said, "A lot of us have played for the old folks many times in the past. This would just be better organized than what we've done before."

"I don't know about the rest of you all," said Ruth, "but just having the opportunity to play in front of an audience has really given me confidence."

"I'll attest to that," said Kate, "after playing in front of people I'm thinking, 'what was I nervous about?'"

139

Ace was not a talkative person unless he had something significant to talk about. "Well, boys and girls," he often started off with that expression, "people often have a tendency to think that they need to look in a large population center to find things of higher quality. This isn't necessarily the case. I'll tell you a true story I heard several years ago. Back when people from big cities first started building retirement homes in north Arkansas and southern Missouri, there was a retired couple from the northeast who were building a house near Mountain Home. Oh, they were building a beautiful place. They had them a well-respected construction company to build according to their desires. Well, they wanted hardwood floors. The contractor said, 'fine, we can do that for you.' They asked, 'where do you get your flooring?' He said, 'why the oak flooring mill in Calico Rock.' They said, 'Well we're going to drive down and look at that mill before we decide anything.' So that's what they did. They drove down there and they looked at that mill. Oh, there was a group of low buildings with rusty corrugated roofing, puddles in the driveways. There were trucks, thirty years old, parked around the place. Well, they thought, 'we're not going to get our flooring from this outfit, we'll order it from a big national dealer.' So they ordered their flooring from a big company in New York State. Then they waited about a month for their flooring to arrive. It came in on the train and it was delivered by truck to their building site, and there were tags on the bundles of flooring that read, 'Hayes Oak Flooring, Calico Rock, Arkansas."

They all had a good laugh.

"That's a true story?" Fred asked.

"It's true," said Ace, "See, most small town people think they have to go somewhere else to see good entertainment, but somebody like Glen Campbell grew up right outside Delight. Over in Howard County lives a guy named Tonk Edwards, one of the best jazz guitar players there is. Oh, I guess I'm just getting carried away, but we've got some great musicians in this group, and if we just do the best we can every opportunity we get, we've put some joy into the world, and nobody can take that away."

Fred said, "Yeah, you know, up in the big cities there are city boys playing old-time country music that they learned from records that were made before most of us were born. At the same time, there are small town kids playing rock and roll that they don't even know where it came from. I guess I'm just saying, 'make a joyful noise.' But enough of this talk, let's play some music."

They played 'Get Along Home Cindy' with the fiddles leading the way. Then they played Shady Grove. Sarah said, "The folks down in Houston loved hearing me sing Hard Times."

"I'll bet they did," said Ace.

Bud said, "I can play that on the keyboard if you guys want to sing it in harmony."

Sarah started with, "Let us pause in life's pleasures and count our many fears, for we all share sorrow with the poor." Bud was playing big major chords so all the singers could hear their parts. Fred, and Kate, and Ruth hummed along. "There's a song that will linger forever in our ears, oh hard times come again no more."

They all sang along at the chorus, "Tis the song, the sigh of the weary, hard times, hard times, come again no more, many days you have lingered around my cabin door, oh, hard times come again no more." In the weeks to come they sang that song in harmony quite often, and the more they sang it the better the harmony sounded.

Chapter 17

By the second week in September the weather started turning cooler. Everyone was happy to know that fall was on its way. One afternoon Irene and Dotty were in the store talking about pumpkins. "I had some friends," Dotty was saying, "that had a garden fenced off with hog wire about three feet high to keep critters out. They had harvested it all except for their pumpkins, of which, they had about eight big ones. Well they had just one hog, named Huey. Well they had some tall grass growing around the place, hadn't mowed it all summer. So they let Huey out so he could eat that grass. They went grocery shopping, and when they came back, there was ol' Huey, asleep inside that fence and those pumpkins were totally gone. He had just knocked that fence down and devoured all those pumpkins, seeds and all." The phone rang and Irene answered it. It was a local woman, Eunice Yardley.

"Irene, I was just trying to reach Billy Fred. He wasn't at his store and I thought you might know where he is."

"I think he went to Texarkana to get supplies. What did you want to see him about?"

"Well, he's got the cutest little storage building that looks an old barn. I just want to know how much he wants for it."

"What can you afford, Eunice?" Irene asked.

"Oh, I could give him about four hundred for it if I could get it delivered," Eunice replied.

Irene said, "Well, that sounds reasonable. I'll make sure he calls you right away when he gets back, and I'll tell him what you said."

"That's fine Irene, thank you so much." said Eunice.

"You're very welcome," said Irene as she hung up the phone. "I wonder how she knew to call here."

"I suppose because everyone around here thinks y'all are a couple," said Dottie, "but it does sound as though Miz Yardley really wants to buy his 'cute little barn."

Billy Fred came driving up right before six o'clock. Irene told him to call Eunice Yardley right away. He told Eunice she could have the storage building for four hundred but he'd have to charge her twenty-five dollars to have the wrecker service in Dequeen move it for her. She thought that sounded reasonable and it was a deal. She met him at his store the next day and the man from the Fina station in Dequeen was there to move it to her place. Then his phone rang. It was Irene. "Hi, baby, how did it go with Eunice?"

"No problem, it was a done deal," said Billy Fred. "I was just thinking, now I don't want to sound presumptuous…" he couldn't quite figure out what to say next. Irene said, "I think I might have an idea what you're trying to say. If people had the phone number here, it wouldn't matter if you were there all the time, we could take the call."

"Well, yeah, that's what happened today, and it was fine. I wondered if you wouldn't mind doing that on a regular basis." said Billy Fred. "And while I'm at it, I just want to say this."

"I'm listening," said Irene.

"Uh, I want us to stay together. Do you know what I mean?" he asked.

"Yeah, I think I do. Let's think about it. Right now I've got some things I need to do before closing time. I love you too, 'bye now."

Dottie was smiling and Irene smiled back. "Life goes on," said Dottie.

"If you'll load the soda-pop in the coolers I'll clean up the coffee bar," said Irene.

"All right," said Dottie. "Now where will we have the ceremony?"

"That's something to think about," Irene replied, "it has to be indoors. Now wait a minute! What ceremony are you talking about?"

Dottie was laughing, "You have to make plans," she said. "What are you going to wear?"

"Oh, please, I need to take a few deep breaths before we go into this." Irene replied. They were both laughing, and they were still giggling when Kenny and Jimbo came through the door.

"What's so funny?" Jimbo wanted to know.

Dottie said, "Oh, it's nothing, your mom can't decide whether to wear white or something more subdued." She started giggling again.

143

"Now cut that out," said Irene.

"Must be a girl thing of some kind," said Kenny, "whatever it is."

Irene said, "It's about long range plans. When we get a few things worked out we'll tell you all about it."

Perry went out to the stable and poured a pound of oats into each horse's feed trough. Then he went out and called the horses. Within two minutes the pinto, Cookie and the bay mare, Star, were walking in his direction, but he couldn't see Gordy. Star and Cookie were in their stalls eating but still no Gordy. "What's going on?" he thought.

He closed Gordy's stall door and started walking toward the pasture. He hadn't gone twenty yards before he saw a tree that had fallen. He rushed toward the tree and saw that Gordy was lying under the top of the tree. It had fallen and the tree top was resting on the barb-wire fence. Gordy was lying next to the fence and was under the tree branches. When Perry got to him, Gordy raised his head with a look of panic in his eyes. Perry knelt down and stroked his neck, "Easy, boy, we'll get you out of here, just take it easy."

He was thinking, "Yeah, *we'll* get you out of here." He knew he needed help. He ran back to the house and called Irene. When she answered the phone he said, "Gordy's got himself hung up between the fence and a fallen tree. I don't know if he's badly hurt, but I could use some help. Loretta's gone to her mother's place. I'll call over there but if your boys are around I could use their help."

Irene called Arlene's place. "Hello, this is Bud."

"Bud, this is Irene, Perry just called and said Gordy's stuck between a fence and a fallen tree. He needs help, can you come?"

Bud said, "Arlene and I will be over as quick as we can. I'll pay him back for helping me. See you over there."

"What's wrong?" Arlene asked.

"Perry called and said Gordy's pinned between a fence and a fallen tree," said Bud.

"We'll need the chainsaw," said Arlene. "I've had cows get in a pinch

144

like that; I hope Loretta's home, she can keep an animal calm better than anyone I know."

Bud retrieved the chainsaw out of the back room and put it in the back of the pickup. Arlene was behind the wheel. Bud got in the shotgun seat and they headed for Perry's place. Irene and her boys were there and Loretta was back from her mother's place when they pulled up to the house. Loretta said, "All of you stay right here. Give me five minutes to get down there, then come on down. But be real quiet and act real calm like we know what we're doing."

They all watched as Loretta walked calmly down toward the fallen tree. When she was almost there she started talking. "Gordy, it's gonna be all right. You just lay still, we're gonna help you out of there. You just take it easy and we'll have you out of there in a minute." It wasn't so much what she said, it was how she said it that made animals trust her. In about three minutes the rest of the folks were around her. She was stroking his neck and telling him to stay calm.

Perry said, "Tell us what you want us to do, honey."

"OK, how many people do we have?" Loretta wanted to know.

"About ten," said Irene. "I've got a couple of granola bars for Gordy."

"Hand them to me," said Loretta.

By that time word had spread and three teenage boys, two teenage girls and three middle aged men were there. At that point Bud said, "Why don't we deploy on both sides of the top of the downed tree. Let's see if we can lift it enough that Arlene can back the pickup under the trunk. Each person can find a stout limb and we'll see if we can raise it up." Five people crawled through the fence and went to the far side of the tree. Arlene drove the pickup down and backed up perpendicular to the tree trunk and pushed in the clutch. "Everyone spread apart and find a stout limb. When I say 'lift', we'll do it together. Everyone ready? One, two, three, LIFT."

The tree rose about two feet and Arlene let out the clutch and backed under the tree trunk. Bud said, "Let 'er down." The tree trunk was two feet higher off the ground.

145

"Loretta said, "We need to cut off a couple of these limbs so we can drag him out from under here. I'll keep him calm 'til we've got the chainsaw going." Arlene started her saw and slowly revved it up. Loretta slowly fed Gordy the granola bars while Arlene started cutting the limbs from the underside of the downed tree. When she'd cut off six branches she turned off the saw.

Kenny said, "The roots on this tree were all rotted away. All it took was a good wind gust to knock it over."

"If somebody was to invent a way to see if that's happening to a tree, they could probably make a lot of money," said Perry.

"OK," said Loretta, "let's have a couple of people get ahold of his front legs and his elbows and pull. That way he can move his hips and wiggle out of here."

"Horses have elbows?" Jimbo asked.

"Right here," said Loretta, touching the upper part of his front leg. "How do you think they can raise their front legs? Sit down on the ground with your back facing away from him and dig your heels into the ground."

A couple of the boys got alongside Gordy's shoulders and pulled him forward. He started working his hips and shoulders until he slid out from under the tree. Then he stood up. He shook himself and grunted. Everyone applauded.

"One more granola bar for Gordo," said Irene as she handed it to him. He chewed with obvious relish.

Loretta said, "Now I want you to understand, Flash Gordon, this wasn't a trick we were teaching you to do by rewarding you with the granola bars. I want you to stay out from under trees when the wind's blowing." Everybody had a good laugh.

Dr. Barnes had arrived. "Let me check him over and see if he's got any injuries." Doc put pressure on the horse in several places to see if he was tender anywhere and if he had any edema. "He seems to be all right," Doc said, "You'd best let him loaf around for the next couple of days. Bud, did you help this ol' boy get back on his feet?"

"Sure did, Doc, I owe him a lot for what he did for me," Bud drawled.

146

The group had another good laugh.

The next afternoon in the store Irene and Dottie were talking. "You know," said Dottie, "the old Legion Hut in Nashville is a good place as any for an indoor event. But you need to book it way in advance."

"I know," said Irene, "we need to call Jake about a month ahead to reserve it. I agree, it's a good place and it's only about fifty miles."

The old Legion Hut was built right after World War I and was constructed of conglomerate rock which was abundant in the area of the Little Missouri River. Before the local Catholic congregation built their own church on the north side of Nashville, they attended Mass in the Legion Hut for nearly forty years. There were local people who thought the Catholics shouldn't be allowed to use the building but they were in the minority. Dottie got Jake on the phone the next afternoon. "Hi, Jake, this is Dottie in Pine Valley. When's the next Saturday the Legion Hut is available?"

"How many people will there be?" Jake asked.

"Are you kidding? The whole population of Pine Valley would fit in the building," Dottie replied. "My friend Irene is getting married, but don't tell that to anybody, it's still in the planning stages."

"You mean she doesn't know if she's pregnant yet?" Jake quipped.

"Now cut that out, I'm just trying to reserve the damn building for a nice quiet get-together."

"Oh, all right, just as long as nothing illegal is going on. Let me see, I think the second Saturday in October is open. Say, how is Doc Barnes doing? I sure miss him."

"Oh, he's doing well. Enjoying his retirement. Ok, put us down for the second Saturday in October, Jake." Dottie ended the call.

"Well," said Dottie, "we've got that taken care of, what's next?"
"Oh, anything and everything," said Irene. "I know, let's put one person in charge of each component of the whole shindig. One person can be in charge of food, one for decorations, and so on."

"Yeah," said Dottie, "that'll work. And we can let the Drifters take care of all the music and dancing and whatever in the line of entertainment. I think we should put Dan Yardley in charge of information. Girl, we're

147

gonna have ourselves a time!"

Dan Yardley was Eunice's husband. He didn't talk much but he was a great organizer. All they had to do was give Dan's number under 'for more information' and he would do the rest.

Bud was helping Fred pull the rear axle out of a Ford pickup. It was about four o'clock and the kids were out of school. Kenny wandered in and sat down on a lard bucket. Bud said, "Hey, Kenny, what's happening?"

"I don't know what to think. I just found out my mom is getting married."

"Wasn't she married when you were born? Why shouldn't she get married again?"

"Well, she didn't even ask me," Kenny groaned.

Fred said, "Like you weren't gonna give her permission?"

"Well, it's not that, she just never said anything about it."

Bud asked, "What does your brother think about it?"

"I don't know," said Kenny, "he didn't say."

Bud said, "Well, it looks to me like you're bothered about not having talked to other family members about their future plans. And that's easily remedied. Just tell your mom you need to talk to her, or you and your brother need to talk to her when she gets a chance. And, I might suggest, talking to her intended partner."

Kenny mused, "You know, you always make it sound simpler when I thought it was more complicated."

"Hand me that half inch ratchet," said Fred "Kenny, are you and your brother friends with Billy Fred?"

"Oh, I guess we are, why?" said Kenny.

"I just think that's a good thing since you're going to be family," Fred replied, "And it occurs to me that ol' Bud here might be getting some ideas in his head of a good opportunity he wouldn't want to miss out on."

"Now just what the heck are you saying, Fred?" Bud wanted to know.

"Oh, I'm just talking about missed opportunities, that's all," Fred replied. They could hear the sound of the phone ringing in the office.

148

"Get that for me Kenny, if you don't mind." Kenny walked into the office.

Kenny called out, "It's for Bud. It's Arlene." Bud walked towards the office.

Fred said, "What do you bet there's some of this opportunity at work, even as we speak." A few minutes later Bud was back.

"Well, I've got to run, Fred. I'll talk to you later," said Bud.

Fred said, "Ok, let me guess, Arlene wants to have a talk with you, right?"

"Oh, no, I'm not going there. You'll just have to wait, along with everybody else." Bud didn't say another word but just kept walking towards Arlene's pickup.

The phone rang again. This time it was Irene telling Kenny to come to the store. When he got there, Billy Fred Driscoll and Jimbo were sitting in lawn chairs out front. Billy Fred said, "Hey Kenny, I was just asking your brother if you'd like to go fishing on Ouachita this Saturday."

"Well, yeah, I'd like to do that. Starting out early?"

"Early would be good, I think," Billy Fred replied, "You all might know of some good spots to fish in."

Jimbo said, "I know a couple of good places close to Shangri La."

"Well my boat is docked at Shangri La, so that makes it convenient. You boys have any tackle?" Billy Fred asked.

"Oh, sure," said Kenny. "We've got some great lures, but if they're not taking lures they'll go for minnows. I'm kind of partial to crappie, but bass fishing is Ok too."

"This is gonna be great," said Kenny. "I didn't know you had a boat, Mr. Driscoll. What kind of boat is it?"

"It's a nineteen foot outboard with a seventy-five horse Evinrude," said Billy Fred. "Did you ever see the movie 'The Rescuers'?"

"Oh yeah," said Jimbo. "It was Bob Newhart and Eva Gabor. And they had this flatboat that was a leaf, and a dragonfly named Evinrude was the motor. Eva Gabor kept saying, 'fahster, Evinwude, fahster."

"That's the one," said Billy Fred.

When Bud arrived back at Arlene's place he wasn't positive but he did

149

have some idea of what she wanted to talk about. Just to have a place to come home to- settle down if you will, had been going through his mind the last two months, and he knew the thought had been there before. He wasn't sure how long, but he knew it was there.

"Hey Babe," she said as she met him at the door. "Sit down here." She pointed toward the couch.

Bud sat down next to her and said, "So you think we need to talk?"

"Yeah, I'm considering moving half of the cows into the north pasture." Arlene replied.

Bud was a little surprised. It wasn't what he expected. He chuckled and closed his eyes. Then he laid his arm across her shoulders. She looked a little bewildered. Then he said, "I think that's a fine idea, I'll help you any way I can."

"But you thought I wanted to talk about something else?" she asked.

"Yeah. I guess it's *my* position I need to explain. You see, just recently, Irene and Billy Fred came to the conclusion that they wanted to stay together. He was having to stay at his storage shed place all day long and he couldn't do other things. And they realized that if people were to just call Irene's store and leave a message, they could get hold of him that way. So then, her boys got wind of the fact their mom was planning to get hitched and they were suddenly surprised. Then, while I was over helping Fred, Mr. Driscoll called to ask Kenny if he and Jimbo wanted to go fishing." Bud paused.

Arlene was nodding her head. "Sounds like the old boy was planning on talking to the kids to see if they had any objections. So, go on, or is that the whole story?"

"Ah, well no, then Fred started ribbing me about letting opportunities get away." Bud paused.

"Mr. Rayburn, are you suggesting that you and I might take the opportunity to get in on the same celebration?"

Bud said, "That about sums it up."

Arlene said, "Sounds like a fine idea to me." She grabbed his shoulders and planted a big kiss on his mouth. "When is this shindig going to be?"

"Don't know for sure, I think we'll find out fairly soon."

"Is this what you really want, Bud?"

150

"It's what I really want," he said with a smile.

Arlene called Irene. "Hey girl, guess what?"

Irene said, "Well let me tell you first. Me and ol' Billy Fred are tying the knot. Don't tell me you're doing the same thing."

"We just need to find out what date you're thinking about and can we turn it into a double whammy."

"Honey, it's a free country, you're welcome to tag along it you're willing to put up with our rowdy friends."

"Any rowdy friends of yours are rowdy friends of mine." They both had a good laugh.

When Kenny and Jimbo found out about Bud and Arlene, any misgivings they had about their mom getting married were forgotten. They wanted to be in on the organizing, so Dottie put them in charge of the food. It was going to be pot luck in any case, with barbecue as the main dish. But it was necessary to divide up the separate courses and they could handle that. When Mr. Yardley got any calls pertaining to the food he turned them over to Kenny and Jimbo. It wasn't the first time there had been barbecue grills set up outside the Legion Hut. The Nashville Walmart was close by, so if anything was overlooked in the organization department it was readily available. It was, obviously, a dress-up occasion, but in southwest Arkansas dress-up is a little different than anywhere else in the world. Men go to church in red suits with cowboy boots or two-tone loafers. Women wearing red dresses adorned with sequins are considered high fashion. Red and white are the colors of the Razorbacks in Fayetteville and the Reddies of Henderson State in Arkadelphia.

Kenny and Jimbo were up early Saturday eating cereal and checking their supply of lures. Then they waited for Billy Fred while they watched cartoons on TV. He finally arrived around six. It was a good hour drive to Lake Ouachita so they had plenty of time to talk on the way. Billy Fred waited for a few minutes before he said anything. Finally he said, "Boys, I guess you know by now your mom and I are planning to get hitched. Now, I realize I can't be your dad- I'm not gonna try to be your dad. I just want to be your friend. Your mom and I both run a business, can we

151

be a business family, do you think?"

"Kenny said, "Yeah, I don't see why we couldn't all work together."

"I agree," said Jimbo, "We'll just help each other."

Billy Fred said, "I know it's hard to imagine, but it won't be any time at all before you boys will be grown up. Then we'll all be adults for many years to come. Are there any questions you all might have?"

"Yeah," said Jimbo, "can I drive the boat when we get up there?" Kenny and Billy Fred both laughed.

They bought two dozen minnows at the marina. The weather was warm. They headed north and found a deep spot fairly close to the shore. They all baited their hooks with minnows and tried to get deep, hoping the bass would be where they expected. Jimbo got the first strike. It took him three minutes to reel it in. When it was up close to the boat Billy Fred netted it for him. It was a three pounder. They stayed in that spot for half an hour and caught four nice bass.

Then they decided to try another spot. Jimbo piloted the boat. They crossed to the south bank, looking for a spot similar to the one they found before. As the day warmed up they didn't get much action. Kenny looked in the bucket for the smallest minnow. He baited his line and it let to down about eight feet. He was hoping to catch a crappie. When he caught one, Mr. Driscoll told them he knew of some areas in the lake where crappie predominated. By mid-afternoon they had lots of crappies to go along with the bass. They filleted the fish at the dock and got a bag of ice to put in Billy Fred's picnic cooler. Their catch would stay cool on the way back home.

"You boys want to get a burger at the café before we head back?" Mr. Driscoll offered.

"Fine with me," said Kenny, "I bet ol' Jimbo will go along with that." His brother nodded.

While they were eating their hamburgers and drinking Sprite, Jimbo said, "Well, Mr. Driscoll, what do you think of our Bud?"

"Oh, I think a lot of Bud, most of the folks in Pine Valley like him. By the way, just call me 'Billy Fred', we can be on first names if we're family. I don't know if you all heard about it, Bud and Arlene are getting married at the same time."

152

"Oh, we knew that," said Kenny, "They put us in charge of food. Anybody who wants to know what food to bring, they call us."

Billy Fred said, "Yeah, I think Arlene found her a first rate guy when Bud came to town, and it was you boys that found him. He'll always have a special connection with your family. You can be sure of that."

As they were driving back home, Billy Fred Driscoll felt like he had connected with Irene's boys really well, and that they were good young men that their mother could be proud of.

Chapter 18

Ronnie Evers had just come home from work when the phone rang. His wife answered, "Hello, this is Lucille."

Cody said, "Ron Evers please."

"Honey, it's for you."

When Ronnie answered, Cody said, "This is agent Carlton with the Texas Bureau of Investigation. I'd like to ask you some questions if you don't mind. Would this evening be convenient?"

"I don't know, do I need a lawyer?"

"That's up to you, sir. Tell you what, why don't I come by and I'll explain what this is in reference to. If I ask you anything you think you need to consult a lawyer about, we'll quit there and I won't ask anything else until you have a lawyer present. Is that all right?" said Cody.

"Yeah, I guess so. You want the address?"

"I've got the address, I'll see you in about ten minutes." Cody turned to Rocky and said, "You ready?"

She said, "Let's go."

When they arrived at the Evers abode, Rocky was the first to go to the door. When Ronnie answered the door she said, "Hi, I'm agent Savage, you must be Mr. Evers."

"Yeah, I was expecting a man."

"Oh, he's coming." Cody arrived at the door shortly. "May we come in?"

"Uh, yeah, come on in." Lucille Evers walked into the room.

Ronnie said, "Honey, this is… what was your name?"

Rocky said, "I'm agent Savage, you can call me Rocky, and this is Cody Carlton. We're both with the Texas Bureau of Investigation."

Lucille said, "Won't you sit down." The two agents sat on the sofa next to Ronnie, and Lucille pulled up a chair.

Cody said, "Like I said on the phone, you can decide if you need a lawyer to represent you, but let me explain what we're doing. By the way, do you have any children?"

"We have a daughter, Lulu, she's not home right now," said Lucille.

"This is in regard to a couple of men you may know- Colin Rayburn and Gino Candiota," said Cody. "They were living around here but then, subsequently moved away. We believe they were, shall we say, pursued by someone who worked for a local uniform service. Do you follow me so far?"

"I think I do," said Ronnie.

"We think you might know something about that," said Cody. "Could we ask you some questions about that, or do you need to be represented by an attorney?"

Lucille said, "Ronnie, if you use a lawyer from the guys that own the laundry service, they're going to be making all your decisions for you."

Ronnie said, "What choice do I have?"

"We can get you a fully qualified attorney that you won't have to pay for, but first I must explain that you may have criminal charges against you. Before I ask you any questions, I need to tell you that if you cooperate with us we don't have to make any charges against you." Cody explained.

"You don't know what these people are like that I work for," said Ronnie

Rocky said, "I think we do, Mr. and Mrs. Evers. But you don't have to stay here. We can help you get relocated a long way from here, get you set up with new jobs and you won't have to deal with these kind of people anymore."

Ronnie and Lucille looked at one another for several minutes.

Cody said, "No matter what happened before, you can decide which side to be on. We'll let you think it over. Tomorrow is Saturday, we'll call you and we can talk some more. Think it over."

When Rocky and Cody were gone, Ronnie looked over at Lucille and shrugged his shoulders. She said, "Well, Baby, the way I look at it, you knew you had to get away from those people if you want live your own life. This way the law will make it easier on us to do that. Lulu will be home soon, we don't have to tell her about it right away, we'll wait until we talk to the law before we tell her the whole story."

"We don't even know the whole story," said Ronnie.

"I'll get you a beer and you can relax and watch TV. I'll fix supper-when Lulu gets home tell her to come talk to me," said Lucille. She was thinking, 'now where would I like to move to?'

Lulu was fourteen. She had average looks, like her mother, and just little bit heavy set. When she got home, Ronnie sent her to the kitchen. Her mother just told her that the family might be moving, soon.

Cody called Pete Bishop at his hotel. "What's the scoop Cody?"

"I think Evers is going to cooperate with us."

"Great. So, what did you tell him?"

Cody said, "We're going to pick up his family early tomorrow and go off to our little get-together. He has a wife and and fourteen year old daughter. Where are we going?"

"Place called Crockett, about an hour's drive from here. I'll do the driving. Did he say if he wanted a lawyer?"

"We told him we'd fix him up with a lawyer, is that a problem?"

"Nah, I'll just bring Sweeney along and tell him he's his lawyer."

Cody and Rocky got to the Evers' around eight o'clock. Lulu was gone to spend the day with her best friends, Tamra and Louise. Lucille asked where they were going.

Rocky said, "a town called Crockett, ever been there?"

Lucille said, "no, but I know it's a small town."

"Exactly," said Rocky, "we want to be somewhere where we don't attract attention. Mr. Bishop and a lawyer named Sweeney are meeting us there."

They got in Cody's car and headed north from Pasadena. When they got on interstate forty-five Mrs. Evers said, "If we wind up relocating it will be harder on our daughter than on us."

"Well it becomes a question of kids wanting to be in touch. It's a little tricky. You don't want the kids to know where she is. You just tell them something vague and say that she'll get in touch with them when she gets moved in to her new home." Cody explained. "However, this is all up in the air at this point. When we get together with Mr. Bishop and Mr. Sweeney at the courthouse we'll be able to make plans and decisions."

"We'll be in a courthouse?" Lucille asked.

156

"Yes ma'am," Rocky answered, "the Houston County Courthouse."

"That's funny," said Ronnie, "You'd think Crockett would be in Crockett County."

Cody said, "No, Ozona is the county seat of Crockett County, and Houston is in Harris County. I know it's strange, but that's one reason why kids learn state history in school."

Crockett is a small town of less than ten thousand. The courthouse is in a square the way most county seats were laid out in the nineteenth century.

"I'll never forget the first time I came to Crockett," Rocky mused. "I was with my dad, and my mom wasn't along. My little sister was so rowdy she'd get her long blonde hair all kinked up with pieces of straw and sticks. Nobody could brush her hair but Mom. She'd start kicking and screaming. She was a holy terror. Well we stopped in Crockett to eat lunch. My old man figured we'd take her to a beauty shop. He told me to walk across the street to a dry goods store and ask a female employee how to get to the closest beauty shop. So the dry goods store lady says, 'Why do you need a beauty shop?' So I say, 'to get my little sister's hair brushed.' So she says, 'Oh, bring her in here, I'll brush her hair.' I had my doubts, but that ol' gal knew how to do it. My little sister never screamed once."

The Houston Co. courthouse was a majestic old building with a broad expanse of concrete steps leading to the front door. Cody parked in front and they entered the building. The man at the front entrance directed them to the county attorney's office. They only waited ten minutes until Bishop and Sweeney arrived. Pete Bishop was carrying a MacDonald's bag. He said, "I took the liberty of buying some lunch, folks."

As they passed around the burgers, Bishop began, "I got assigned to this case back last summer. My interest has mainly been in a person we had in witness protection. The individual that was in protection was pursued, which is a violation of federal law. We also know that he was kidnapped, which is a state and federal offence, and we believe an attempt was made on his life. All of these offences are felonies punishable by maximum life

157

imprisonment. Now, it's our belief that Mr. Evers was hands-on involved in these violations. However, we also believe he didn't act alone which gives us reason to forgo direct prosecution if we can get cooperation from Mr. Evers to further our investigation. Mr. Sweeney can speak for Mr. and Mrs. Evers about any of these charges. Any questions?"

Ronnie said, "Can Mr. Sweeney explain what my options are?"

Sweeney said, "What Mr. Bishop is saying is that what we're interested in finding out about, is who runs this operation. In other words, the people Colin Rayburn testified against and who he was supposed to have been protected from. The government is willing to waive those felony charges, provided they get full cooperation, and they're willing to give protection to you, Mr. Evers, like they did with Mr. Rayburn."

Ronnie Evers said, "I get your point. Boy, that protection didn't hold up too good, did it."

Lucille said. "Ronnie, I think you ought to explain to them about what you had to do with that."

"Is that OK Mr. Sweeney?" Ronnie asked.

"That would be good, because we need to get to the nitty gritty about this," said Doug Sweeney.

"Well, Colin and I were working for the laundry service. A detective guy talked to us about some unlawful business practice and they wanted somebody to witness for the state. I told 'em I couldn't do it because I got a family and I didn't want to put them in danger."

"But what about Colin?" Pete Bishop wanted to know.

"Well, Colin didn't have no family," Ronnie replied.

Mr. Bishop said, "So Colin was a state witness?" Ronnie nodded. "Now let me ask you this. Did you know that the laundry service, no pun intended, was a money laundering operation?"

Evers said, "I'm not sure I understand."

Bishop said, "It means the business wasn't there to make a profit. They put money they'd gotten illegally into it and showed a profit from that same money. All they had to do was to cook the books and come out with money that looked like they earned it. Now, we didn't know about the money laundering back when Colin testified about the fair market violations. But did it seem like there was something fishy about the way they ran that company?"

"Well, now that you mention it, that payroll check I got every Friday was kinda funny," Ronnie replied.

"In what way, Mr. Evers?" Bishop asked.

Ronnie said, "Well they took out for federal and state tax and they took out for insurance."

"What kind of insurance?" Pete Bishop asked.

"Well, like legal insurance. So if you ever got in trouble with the law it would pay for a lawyer," said Ronnie.

Cody said, "Seems like if you got in legal trouble it would be because of the way they were running the company. In which case it would pay to protect them more than you."

"It would seem," said Bishop. "Now didn't you go looking for Colin Rayburn after he left town?"

"Yeah, I guess I did." said Evers.

"But that wasn't your idea, was it?" said Lucille Evers.
"No it wasn't," said Ronnie.

"Whose idea was it?" Bishop wanted to know.

"I don't know whose idea it was, but my boss said I could get some overtime if I went to Missouri to see Gino." Ronnie replied.

"And your boss was?" Bishop asked.

"Furry. Johnny Furumo," Ronnie replied.

"So you went to Missouri to see Gino Candiota?" Ronnie nodded.

"Actually, I was just supposed to check on Gino, but when I got there I was looking on the wall next to the phone and I saw 'CR, and a number." said Evers.
"I couldn't remember the whole number but it was a three one six prefix."

"And then you did what?" Bishop asked.

"I came home," Ronnie replied.

"And then what happened?" Pete Bishop asked.

"Furry sent me to Wichita, Kansas. He told me to go to a shopping center where they had a music store and be there on Saturday afternoon. I went to a place they call Town East. Colin was playing an electric piano out in front of a music store," Evers related.

159

"So how did you find out where he lived?" asked Bishop.

"I followed him home," Ronnie replied.

"For the sake of saving us all time and effort," said Bishop, "why don't you go on with your story up until the point where you kidnapped Rayburn."

Ronnie said, "Mr. Sweeney, am I gonna incriminate myself if I do that?"

Doug Sweeney said, "You've already done that several times over already. Since you've been offered and accepted protection, you need to comply with it to hold up your end of the bargain."

Lucille Evers said, "I think it's coming down to making a choice between these folks and the ones you've been working for ever since we came here. You did what Furry told you to and what he told you was against the law and he knew it."

"Yeah, I guess you're right," said Ronnie, "but what I want to know is, are my family and I gonna be safe from those people after all this?"

Pete Bishop said, "I think Mr. Sweeney has been in on some of these immunity and witness protection deals in the past. But you need to understand you're not going to be testifying in court against anybody."

"That's right," said Sweeney. "Typically, if we relocate somebody they'll have a choice of several places to live."

Cody added, "Yeah, but don't be playing music at an indoor mall." Even Lucille had a laugh on that one.

Ronnie said, "Ok, I found out where Colin was living. He was in an apartment and was driving a Pontiac. I had another guy with me and we carried Colin off in his own car."

Bishop asked, "Who was this other guy and how did you get him in the car?"

"They call him Big Bird, his last name is B-Y-R-D. He's a really big man. I don't know his real first name. Furry told me to hit Colin over the head but we didn't do that. I had nothing against Colin, I didn't want to hurt him. We just dragged him out of bed in the middle of the night and wrapped duct tape around his hands and feet and his mouth to keep him quiet. Then we carried him out and put him in the back of his car. Furry also told me to take all his IDs, so I took everything out of his wallet. Then I put a twenty dollar bill in it, and put it back in his pocket."

Bishop frowned, "Why did you do that? I mean the twenty bucks."

"Oh, I made a bet with him on the Super Bowl and he won, so I was just paying him back. See, I didn't think the Cowboys would win back-to-back championships, but they did."

"And you don't have any idea what Mr. Byrd's first name is?" Bishop asked.

"I think it might be either Gary or Jerry," said Ronnie.

"I see," said Bishop. "So where did you take him?"

"Furry said to take him across a state line and into a rural area. Then we should throw him off a bridge," Ronnie related. "He didn't say which bridge so we looked for a bridge that wasn't over water and wasn't too high."

Rocky said, "You know, it sounds as though they wanted you to bump him off, but instead you gave him a break."

Sweeney said, "It would seem so. Anyway, Mr. Bishop has a list of some relocation addresses you can choose from."

Bishop said, "That's right, and they all are a pretty good distance from this area. Also, it's up to you to decide how you want to 'cover your tracks', so to speak. You probably want to tell a few people that you're moving away, that way you wouldn't cause suspicion. Now I've got one more question, Mr. Evers. What did you do with Mr. Rayburn's car?"

"We drove it back to his place in Wichita and we drove Big Bird's car back to Houston," said Ronnie.

"Very well, Mr. Evers, we've got some papers for you to sign. Then you and your wife can go through this list of addresses and decide where your new home will be," Pete Bishop told them. "We'll check with you from time to time and make sure you're getting along OK."

Mr. Sweeney said, "One more thing before we go. Sometime in the future we have to have a court hearing. We'll contact you and let you know when and where that will be."

"A court hearing?" Ronnie looked surprised.

161

"Yes, just a formality we have to do. There will be a judge. We'll show him the documents of the agreement we made with you. He'll look at the documents and he'll ask you if you've read these agreements and if you've signed them."

In the end, the Evers' moved to Edina Minnesota, where Ronnie got a job driving a delivery truck for an auto parts dealer. Lucille waited tables at an Olive Garden restaurant. As promised, the FBI stayed in touch with them, which gave the government the opportunity to get more information from Ronnie if need be. The conversation at the meeting in Crockett, Texas had been tape recorded.

Pete Bishop had a meeting with Bud in Pine Valley and played the tape for him. He told Bud that he still had the option of suing Ronnie Evers in civil court if he wanted to. After thinking it over, Bud felt that if anybody else from Starr's operation, besides Ronnie, had done the dirty work, he probably wouldn't be alive. In the long run they realized that now Ronnie would know exactly what it felt like to escape from a gang of outlaws.

Bud called Dr. Barnes and told him that he'd heard the tape of Ronnie Evers' interrogation. Doc said, "I think it might be helpful if you and Albert James and I were to sit down and chat about that." Bud agreed to that. When the three of them got together at Doc's place he had a question for Bud.

"Did it ring a bell when you found out the name of your kidnapper?"

"It did, vaguely, but I still don't have a clear memory of the event. I can remember waking up in the creek bottom and I can remember being in the apartment in Wichita, but the space in between is all blank."

Doc said, "Well, there was probably too much trauma for your brain to hold onto."

"Is that an expected result?" Judge James wanted to know.

"It seems to be," said Doc, "in many cases you hear about."

Bud said, "It was a mistake to give my phone number to Gino. This wouldn't have happened if I hadn't done that."

"Well, the FBI didn't warn you about such things. They should have, but maybe that experience will help somebody in the future."

162

Nobody said anything for several minutes. Then Bud said, "You know, there's something I've often thought about. We talk about, 'what are the chances of this, or what are the chances that?' Here we are on a small planet near a small star. There's no life, intelligent or otherwise for hundreds of light years in any direction. You could have been a hundred pounds of carbon anywhere in the universe. We've all won the cosmic lottery. Whether it was 'intelligent design'
or pure chance, the fact that we're even here, the odds against it are astronomical. You know what I mean?"

"You're a wise man, Bud," said the judge.

"I agree" said Dr. Barnes, "he does have unusual insight."

163

Chapter 19

Barry Duncan had just come home from school when the phone rang. Mr. Duncan answered it. "Hi, this is Rocky, your friendly neighborhood FBI agent. I just found out that your friend, the keyboard player, is getting married this weekend."

"That's good to hear, where is this happening?"

"I thought you might ask that," Rocky replied. "It's about three hundred miles from here, but the location has to be in confidence. Now, if you folks want to go we can arrange that. Alternatively, if Barry wants to go, I'll be driving up myself and he can ride with me."

"All right, let me ask him if he wants to do that." He asked Barry, "Do you want to go to Colin's wedding? He's getting married this weekend. You could ride there with Rocky, the FBI agent."

"Oh, sure Dad, I'd love to go."

"Rocky, I'm putting Barry on." He handed the phone to his son.

One of Pine Valley's entrepreneurs was a man named Delbert Tinsley. Delbert made barbecue grills from used oil drums. They weren't very different from commercially made grills, but they had lots of capacity. At the double wedding at the Legion Hut in Nashville, Arkansas there were three of Tinsley's grills, but they wound up using only two of them. Almost half the population of Pine Valley was in attendance and they consumed in excess of two hundred pounds of barbecued ribs.

Music would be provided by the Pine Valley Drifters. Since it was a rather large gathering they needed amplified sound. Among the group there were several amps, mics, and monitors. Ace had a PA system that he had used only once, but it was perfectly adequate for their needs. It was just a small problem to transport the wedding guests to the Howard Co. seat. There were plenty of vehicles among them and they did quite a bit of car-pooling.

There was tall grass and weeds on the grounds surrounding the Legion Hut. Jim Tanner was able to borrow a tractor with a bush hog and cut them down. Then he sprayed insecticide over the whole area. Disease carrying ticks are a big problem in that part of the country.

Neither of the brides were dressed in white. Arlene and Dottie found a nice pair of red frontier pants from the Walmart in Texarkana and a beautiful ruffled shirt with embroidered flowers from Dillard's. Arlene already had a red jacket. It needed to be let out just a little, but Mrs. Tinsley did it for her as a gift to the bride. The consensus of the people at the wedding was that both of the brides were was absolutely stunning.

Irene's outfit was a peach colored dress. It had short sleeves and a wide neck, with a knee-length skirt. It came from Maurice's in Arkadelphia. She had seen it a few weeks before and admired it but, it seemed too expensive at the time. But since she was getting married she had a better reason for spending the money.

Jim's deuce and a half truck easily held all the sound equipment and a lot of wedding guests. After unloading the equipment and a few other passengers, Jim proceeded to the local Walmart and then to Fred's to pick up a few necessities that weren't available elsewhere. Billy Fred had asked Jim to pick up some saw palmetto at Fred's. As soon as he entered the store the clerk, named Kitty, asked him if she could find something for him.

"I'm looking for saw palmetto."

"I'm glad you came in here, Walmart is out of it," she replied. "I'll show you where it is."

Jim had no idea what the stuff was used for. "You get a lot of call for saw palmetto?"

"Sure, ever since folks found out it's good for BPH. Here it is, sir," she said pointing to the jar in the pharmaceutical section. "If you used a prescription drug it would cost over eight dollars a pill."

"Wow, no wonder my friend wants it, thank you very much."

Jim began thinking about all the stuff he had to haul up from Pine Valley and that it would take just as much time to haul it all back. A phrase came to mind, 'keep it simple, stupid.' He promised himself he would pass that thought along to the rest of the throng who would be here when the nuptials were taking place.

Sarah called Maggie to see if she had come up with any ideas for the

165

song about Bud. Maggie said, "I don't know, girl, right now I'm working on a big pile of German potato salad. Why don't you drop over and we'll see if we can find some words- two heads are better than one."

"That sounds like a good idea," Sarah replied. "I'll see you in a few."

When Sarah arrived, Maggie handed her a peeler and the two women began skinning a bunch of Yukon Golds. "All right," said Maggie, "What have we got so far?"

"We've got, 'When I first came to Pine valley, I was a man without a name, didn't know where I was going, or the place from where I came."

Maggie said, "All right, I'll try to come up with another line." Maggie didn't say anything for several minutes. "Ok, how about, 'Oh the people in Pine Valley, they tried to make me feel at home. They were kind and they were friendly, I wouldn't face the world alone."

"Yeah, girl," Sarah said, "I'll get the next one. How about a chorus at this point? Take me back to old Pine Valley, that's the place I want to be. Where nobody is a stranger, Forevermore, it's home to me."

Maggie said, "Hey, it's a song. We've got a verse and a chorus, from here on we'll just add more verses."

"All right," said Sarah, "one more I just thought of, 'Quarter mile from Oklahoma, at the end of a black top road, it's rich in small town beauty, eight seven o's the area code."

"Ok, it's a real song now. The next time we jam we'll sing it for the group and they can help us add to it," said Maggie.

"How many of these taters are we gonna need?" Sarah asked.

Maggie said, "Enough for two big bowls. That's what I'm aiming for. There'll be a whole lot of food, you know how these people are."

"Yeah, I know," said Sarah. "That reminds me of that story about different religions. This teacher asked these kids to bring a symbol of their religion. This Jewish boy says, 'I'm Jewish and this is my Star of David.' Another boy says, 'I'm Catholic and this is my rosary.' A little girl says, 'I'm Presbyterian and this is my casserole dish."

Maggie laughed, "That's pretty good. I'll tell that one at the next jam."

Rocky drove over to the Duncan home on Friday afternoon. Barry appeared at the door when she entered the driveway. He had his fiddle case in one hand and small backpack in the other. She opened the trunk and helped him stow his stuff inside. "Got everything? I'll have a word with your folks before we go." Barry led the way through the door off the garage. Linda Duncan was in the kitchen. "Well, I guess we're ready to take off. It's about three hundred miles and I'll have him call as soon as we get there."

His mom said, "Be good now, I know you'll be glad to see Colin." She said to Rocky, "If you don't make it back by Monday, it'll be ok, his teacher will understand."

Once they were in the car and fastened their seatbelts, Rocky handed Barry a package of Twizzlers licorice. "Give this to Colin, it can be my wedding present."

"There weren't supposed to be any presents, but I'm giving him a flashlight." said Barry.

As they pulled out onto the street, Rocky said, "We'll be on interstates most of the way, but when we get to the border I'll let you navigate for me."

"Which border is that?" Barry asked.

"They call it the Arklatex," Rocky replied, "where Arkansas, Louisiana, and Texas come together."

"Good, I've always wanted to see that country." Barry said. He watched the businesses along the highway as they rolled by. He was happy that he was going to see Colin again, and he was happy to be traveling and seeing places he'd never been to before. He felt a fondness for Rocky that he couldn't really explain. Maybe it was because she was a grown woman but she was much younger than his female teachers. He thought it might be fun, when there was music at the wedding, he might ask her to dance.

Barry asked Rocky, "I guess they know who it was that abducted Colin, will he go on trial?"

"Actually he was more important to us as a source of information," Rocky explained. "The court gave him immunity from prosecution in exchange for that information. He really didn't want to harm Colin. He

167

was just sort of a naïve guy who got involved with the mob and then found it impossible to get out of it. He's going to start over in a new location and he knows not to get involved with any shady characters."

"Whew, it really got complicated for him, didn't it," Barry replied.

"Yes, if you ever take a course in the sociology of human antisocial behavior, you learn about these families where several generations make a living in crime," said Rocky.

"Like the Godfather?" Barry asked.

"Yeah, that's the most famous one, but there are lots of other ones as well," said Rocky. "Unfortunately, this guy named Hoover, who was the director of the FBI from its very beginning, refused to believe that organized crime even existed. The agency didn't start going after mobsters until Hoover was about to retire. But ever since then it's one of our biggest operations."

There were several inhabitants of the Pine Valley community who got to the wedding on their motor-bikes. Johnny Steel and his wife Sally Jean rode in on his Harley. The couple were heavy enough that it took a very large machine to carry them. The driveway of their home, which was just east of Irene's store, was paved with flattened beer cans. It was a simple way to cover the mud. Every beer Johnny drank, he just tossed the can out the front door. It would eventually be smashed flat. Bud had at one time calculated that Johnny's driveway consisted of over fifty dollars-worth of aluminum.

A time of eleven AM was set as the meet-and-greet part of the celebration. The Pine Valley Drifters decided to not make any decisions about who, what, or when to play any music. That did not include *not* playing. There was a small PA system and two microphones. Various members had amps as necessary. One for the keyboard was necessary. Kenny and Jimbo arrived at ten and the first thing they did was start the coals. Before long the inviting aroma of hickory and mesquite filled the air. The weather report was for widely scattered showers. They would've all loved to know just how widely they'd be scattered. As the parking lot began to fill, the inhabitants of Pine Valley began to fill the Legion Hut. Southwest Arkansas has its own standards of clothing styles for dress-up occasions. But this was wedding and barbecue. The clothing style was everything from barbecue style to wedding style. The predominant color was red, but the shades of red were everything from deep burgundy and maroon to international safety red. As Emily Dickinson once said, "I found the words to every thought I ever had but one- And that defies me as a hand did try to chalk the Sun- For races nurtured in the dark, how would your own begin? Can blaze be shown in Cochineal- or noon in Mazarin?" Many of the men wore red sport coats, and two-tone loafers. The red dresses worn by several of the women were adorned with their initials embroidered and decorated with sequins. Cowboy shirts and boots had become popular and were worn by both men and women, but there were more feminine versions for the ladies, with ruffles and embroidery.

They could have had just one minister perform both ceremonies at once. They didn't do that. Arlene's church was a Methodist church in Horatio. Irene and Billy Fred's church was a Baptist church in Dequeen. Both pastors really wanted to be included and so they were. Irene believed in the concept, "When in doubt, be inclusive."

It was a good thing that Fred's friends, James and Margaret, brought a pile of snacks, including grapes, pretzels, tortilla chips and diced veggies, because the Drifters were hot to start playing as soon as enough of them were there to make a quorum. Ace was sawing on his fiddle like there was no tomorrow. He started off with the Gold Rush, then went into Devil's Dream, Sally Gooden and the Pig Ankle Rag before he stopped to eat a few grapes and pretzels. Dottie was keeping a close watch on the punch bowl. It was filled with Sprite, lime sherbet and pineapple juice. There were a few of the good ol' boys who would have spiked it with liquor if they had the chance. But there were kids and Baptists here and the word had been spread that if anyone wanted to imbibe they had to do it behind the oak and gum trees at the edge of the parking area.

When Dexter got there they began doing some waltzes with Dexter playing chords on the guitar. Ace was certain that there would be a lot of older people who liked to dance, and waltzes were what they liked to dance to.

169

When Maggie and Fred got there Dexter switched to the flute since there was rarely a shortage of guitars. Then Charles wandered in carrying his bass and Sarah arrived soon after. From then on the musicians didn't stop playing except for a minute or two when they got into a conversation about some shared memory. Sarah was nearly always in on the conversation. If there was ever anyone who hadn't heard the story about her tossing a couch cushion into a tuba she made sure they heard it.

Both couples were in the building by eleven. So were the two ministers. The Baptist pastor was James Munns, the Methodist pastor was Wesley Hillman. Most of the guests belonged to either a Baptist or Methodist church, but a dozen different denominations were represented, including a few Catholics and Jews.

Dave and Donna Peterson were there early. They loved to dance, especially if it was a waltz. Billy and Susan Jeeter were there. Billy had brought his guitar, but he and Susan loved to dance whenever there was music. Doc and Ruth Marie Smith, Richard and Sharon Gray, and Larry and Angel Cross, would arrive later. They were older couples that had been dancers from the time they were teenagers. The hard core dancers were dressed like they would be for church. Most of the rest of the guests were dressed more casually.

Rocky drove out of Texarkana up I-thirty and turned off at Fulton, then she came through Mineral Springs to Nashville. "Well, we're almost there, Barry, remember not to let on that I'm an officer and that we came from Texas."

"Oh, I won't forget. I kind of hope there's a lot of people there and we won't stand out too much."

Rocky pulled into the parking lot and they continued up the steps to the front door. Barry had his fiddle case in one hand and a small gift-wrapped flashlight in the other hand. There were maybe thirty people outside under the pine trees. Dottie met them when they came inside. Rocky said, "Hi, I'm Rocky and this is Barry. I know there's not supposed to be presents but is there a place to park these little gift-wrapped items?"

Dottie said, "I'll put them in a grocery bag I've got for the couples.

Barry, if you're who I think you are, go on over and see Bud. He'll be over close to the other musicians."

As Barry approached he suddenly said, "COLIN, it's good to see you."
Bud lifted the boy up and said, "Barry, you're a sight for sore eyes. How are your folks?"

"They're fine," Barry said as Bud set him down. "They couldn't come but they sent their best. I rode up with this lady, meet Rocky."
"So you're Rocky," said Bud, "I want to thank you for what you've done."

"Just doing my job, and it was a real treat to drive this young man to your wedding," she replied.

Wesley Hillman was trying to get their attention. "If everyone will face this way and keep their voices down we can proceed with the ceremony." The music stopped when Ace raised his foot. Arlene was beaming. Bud was wearing black Levis with a red plaid shirt and a bolo tie. Wesley said, "We're here to unite this couple, Bud and Arlene, into a marriage. What this meant to our ancestors, down through the ages, was that these individuals were bonded to each other and neither of them were available to anyone else. Will the couple take each other's hands and state their vows. Arlene first."

Arlene said, "Since I first met this man, I knew that if he were willing, I would want to share the rest of my life working with him, and living with him."

Bud said, "Since I first met this woman I've felt like I had a chance to have a home and a partner that I've needed all my life. I'm willing, Arlene, if you are."

Wesley said, "Are there any objections?" A few seconds later he said, "I now pronounce you husband and wife." Everyone cheered.

A few feet away were Irene and Billy Fred. Irene was dressed in the dress she had bought in Arkadelphia. Billy Fred was wearing a grey double breasted suit that he had owned for years but it was newly cleaned and pressed. His tie was Razorback red.

Jim Munns said, "We're gathered here, I guess, for several reasons. One of which is so Irene and Billy Fred can get married. I appreciate what

171

brother Wesley said about the ancient roots of marriage, I agree with that. Let me ask for a statement from this whole congregation. Anyone who is willing to support this couple in their desire to have a lasting elationship, please answer, 'amen." There was a loud amen. "Well then, Billy Fred and Irene, do you take each other to be permanently together with the support of everyone gathered here?"

They both said, "I do."

Jim said, "Then I pronounce you husband and wife." A roar went up from the crowd. Then the Drifters started playing Wild Mountain Thyme, and the Petersons were the first couple to start waltzing. Soon the whole room was full of dancing couples. Bud was waltzing with Arlene when he looked over at the door and saw Bobby and his grandmother, Viola, standing there.

He said, "Honey, let's go welcome our friends." They started in that direction, then Bobby saw them coming. He had a big smile on his face. "We tried to get here sooner, but we ran into a lot of traffic between Tulsa and here."

"It's great to see you," said Bud, "get yourselves some food and join the party."

Sarah was singing the Tennessee Waltz and the dancers were at it again. After that, Sarah asked for everybody's attention. When the noise subsided she said, "Now this is a special surprise for our Bud. I don't know what to call it- maybe 'Pine Valley Homecoming.' It's to the tune of When First Unto this Country." Sarah started singing, "When I first came to Pine Valley, I was a man without a name. Didn't know where I was going, or the place from where I came. Oh, the people in Pine Valley they made me feel at home. They were kind and they were friendly, wouldn't have to face the world alone. Take me back to old Pine Valley, that's the place I want to be, where nobody is a stranger, forevermore, it's home to me. Quarter mile from Oklahoma, at the end of a black top road. It's rich in small town beauty, eight seven oh's the area code." Everyone applauded for Sarah.

Bobby and Viola, and also Barry Duncan and Rocky, were standing close to Bud and Arlene. Barry said, "I hope they don't play that song on the radio, it would give away Colin's whereabouts."

Rocky said, "Oh, we aren't worrying about that song, it won't go far

172

from here. We've got people breathing down the neck of every person in that south Texas mob. And we're far enough from Houston we might as well be on the east coast."

Bud said, "I've got to get in touch with Gino and Millie, they're the only ones who didn't make it. By the way, do you see all these people? This is my family and my neighborhood. I think, maybe, on that chorus it can say, 'Come on back to old Pine Valley. That's the place I want to be. Where nobody is a stranger. Forevermore, it's home to me."

www.ingramcontent.com/pod-product-compliance
Lightning Source LLC
Chambersburg PA
CBHW051518170626
46811CB00002B/879